George Washington Johnson

Autobiography & Poems of George Washington Johnson 1893

George Washington Johnson

Autobiography & Poems of George Washington Johnson 1893

ISBN/EAN: 9783337121563

Printed in Europe, USA, Canada, Australia, Japan

Cover: Foto ©Raphael Reischuk / pixelio.de

More available books at **www.hansebooks.com**

Autobiography.

of

Poems.

of

George. Washington. Johnson.

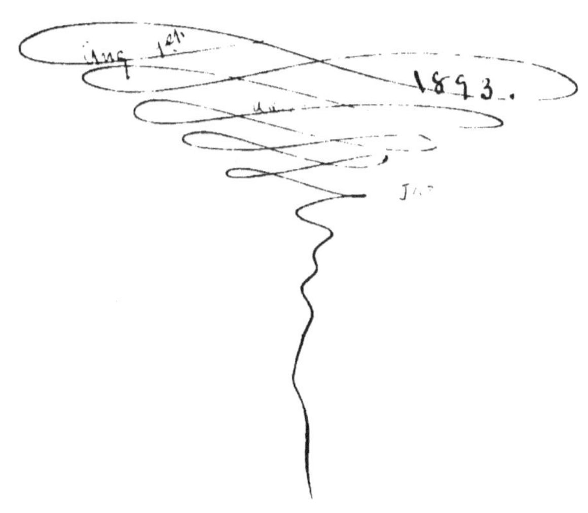

Blessing (J.S.)   41
"   (W McB)   43
Blessing Meeting (Minutes)   44
Burlesque   193, 125, 93, 77
Birth Day for a friend —   99
Birth Day 250 210 157, 123, 93, 188
Bygone Years   186
Back agains   225
Birth Day 66   278 272
Boyhood   280

Dixie
Darenny be true to me
Dollars and Dimes
Dollar or two
Dance on the Brain
Deseret

God Bless our Home
Good Bye
God Bless The Children
Going Down The Hill
Guessing

Happy Days of Yore
Home is still Home
Hope
Home again

January 12th
Jotting By the Way
July 24 1884
July 31 1851 (m.l.f.) Born
June 13 1881
Joseph Smith The Prophet

Little Merry Mormons
Loneliness
Lauras Birth Day

14

My Mother 127, 74, 71
" Wife 72 73
" Sister Esther 201 200 75 78
" Dear old Coat 216 94
" Mothers Ring 102
" Children 110
Mormon Creed 124
My Brave Steed 137
Mothers Birth Day 147
May we not then part as friends 208
Musing (For Old Folks Day) 246
My Lot 266

Never give up
New year,

154
220 <

Reverie
Reality
Religion   (semi
Reflection
Retrospection

Spring
Spring (a Burlesque)
Six Little Graces
Sweet Rose
Sabbath Morning
Send for mother
Sad Memories
Sadness
Seed Circulars
Stencil Circulars
Sweet Deseret   (Er— Italy
Stars and Stripes (In the ladies)

23

Valentinus   210 192

Yankee Doodle

I was Born in the township of Pomfret County of
Chautauque State of New York on the 19th Day of
February in the year 1823 My fathers Name was
Ezekiel My Mothers Maiden Name was Julia Hills
Of my fathers ancestors I know but little
They were Born & Married in the State of Mass=
=achusetts and in the year 1812 with Seven
Children Mooved to the western part of New York
then a New Country where they settled and
Raised a family of Sixteen (16) Children Nine (9)
Sons and (7) Seven Daughters My Mother was a
Devout Presbyterian and Raised Her family in
Strict observence of the Precepts laid down in
the Bible She was Loved & Respected by all
Who knew Her She Died at Council Bluffs
Iowa a firm Believer in the Doctrines taught
By Joseph Smith. During the winter of 1831 My
Brother Joel and a young man by the Name
of Almon W Babbitt Came from Ohio and Bro-
with them the Book of Mormon, other Elders
Soon followed and the Result was that my
Mother and some of Her Children were Baptised
About this time Elder James Brackenbury
then on a Mission was taken Sick at our House
after a short Illness Died and was Buried
at Laona Two of my Brothers (Seth and Daniel)
felt an Impression that the Body would be
Disturbed and Determined to Spend the Night
at the grave On arriving Near they Discovered
two men opening the grave which they had
Nearly accomplished As soon as they were
Discovered they fled My Brothers Pursued them
and Caught one of them But Nothing was Ever
Done to Bring them to Punishment

A Little Previous To this time my oldest
Sister (Nancy) was thrown from a Horse and
Broke Her Hip Bone so near the joint that all
the Doctors was Decided it Could not be set
and Told Her She would Never Have the use of
that Limb again or be able to walk without Crutches
when the Elders began to Preach Miracles Many
people said when Nancy is Healed & throws Bye
Her Crutches we will Believe In the spring of
1833 we moved To Kirtland Ohio where the
Saints were then Gathering Here we became
Acquainted with the Prophet Joseph Smith and
all of the First authorities of the church And
here we witnessed the Falling of the Stars (Meteors)
on the Night of Nov 13th 1833 and The Building
and Dedication of the Kirtland Temple Here I with many
others attended the Hebrew School the Jewries in
the Temple Here on the 9th Day of april 1836 I
with my Brother William were Baptised By
Elder Samuel Bent and confirmed by Joseph
Smith and Received our Patriarchal Blessing
under the Hands of Joseph Smith Sen the First
Patriarch of the church Here also my sister Nancy
who had never walked a step without her
Crutches for Several Years was Healed by
lay the laying on of Hands and Never
used Her Crutches afterwards Here after a
Serious Illness we Buried Four (4) members

1838
Kirt Camp

From Kirtland Ohio In the Spring (July) of 1838 We started for Missourie in what was Known as the Kirtland Camp Consisting of all the Poor Still Remaining at Kirtland And all who were able and willing to Help them Our company Consisted of about Eight Hundred Souls (800) Nerly all in poor Circumstances With Sixty (60) wagons Our Trip was a Very Hard Trying Trip as we were often without Food and There was Much sickness in our Camp At Dayton Ohio we stopped For a while to work on the National Turnpike and give the Sick a chance to Recover While here my Mother & Brother made a trip to Cincinnati to visit His sister, and other Kindred During our Stay here Threats were made that we Should not pass through Mansfield alive (a little Town on our Route) But when we were Ready we Started along in Close Procession the women Driving the Teams and the men walking along side On Nearing the Town we were Met by Two (2) Horsemen who Rode Down Each Side of our Column Seeming to be Counting the wagons &c as they passed along after Satisfying Themselves they Returned to the Town Where a Large Crowd were Collected Fireing Cannon Beating Drums & Seeming to be Much Excited But we passed through & was not molested We afterwards Learned that The Horse men had given the Crowd assembled a Very Exagerated amount of our Numbers and Armament On Reaching Springfield Ills

1838 Samuel Hale Died Leaving A sick wife and One Daughter in our Care Here a Council was Held & it was Decided to Leave the Sick

Here for the present My Brothers Joel Joseph
And the Rest of our Families (Except Benjamin)
were Detailed To Remain with them to take
Care of the Sick. Through the winter following
there was Much Sickness My Mother and My-
=Self were very near Dying with Typhoid fever
Sister Hale Died leaving a Daughter (Maryann)
Whom my mother adopted. We Remained at
Springfield nearly Two (2) years During which
time the Saints were Driven from Missourie.
and Had Commenced Settling at a Place Called
Commerce - (afterwards Nauvoo) - In Hancock. Co. Ills,
on the Rapids of the Mississippi. In the Spring
of 1839 we again Started westward to gather with
the Saints But when we arrived within Twenty (20)
Miles of Commerce It was thought best to Remain
there and Build a Town at a place Called
Perkins Settlement. Land was Purchased and
a Town laid off and Called Ramus (a Branch)
afterwards it was Changed to Macedonia.
We Remained Here about Four (4) years During
which time > My youngest Brother Amos Died.
My Sisters Mary. Esther. My Brother Joseph and
Myself were Married, During the year.
1843 The Mob Broke out Burned Houses Destroyed
Property & Drove the Saints from Place to Place
Joseph & Hyrum Smith were Imprisoned in
Carthage Jail and on the 27th of June 1844

Into the 25th Quorum of Seventies, In June 1844
I moved to Nauvoo, For some time my health
was Very poor and I made up my mind.
to go to the southern country to try to improve
It by Traveling, In the Spring of 1845 I started
For Tennessee where my wifes People were living.
where I arrived safely after a tedious Journey
of several weeks, Here I Remained through the
Summer, And about the First of October Started
back to Nauvoo where I arrived about the last
of the month where I Remained through the
winter, My health Continued poor and not
being able to Labor I Concluded to try traveling
again & again Started for Tennessee where I
again spent 1st and Born winter and in Apr. 1847
again Started for Nauvoo Taking with us
my wifes sister & Her Husband Persons all 50 During my
Absence The saints at Nauvoo had been much
Persecuted by the mob and after a severe
Battle Had been Driven from their Homes
and all their possessions at Nauvoo and all
the settlements arround and were settling in
the western part of Iowa, My Father died
on the 13th of Jan 1848, The times looked Very
Dark and Gloomy, During the next summer
and following winter I Remained at Nauvoo
Exhibiting the Temple to Visitors in connexion
with my Brother in law David T. LeBaron until
it was Burned which Happened on the Night
of Nov 19th 1848 and as a Very Incorrect
account of its Burning has been Published
I will here Insert my account of it.
During the year 1848 David T. Le Baron
and myself were Engaged in Exhibiting the Nauvoo

Temple to Strangers He attended it one day
and I the Next, Generaly, on the 18th day of
November I was taking a party through We
had been to the Top & Returned as far as the
Second story when I Heard Voices Below.
Leaving my Company I Ran Down to the
Main Room below Where I found the Door
Partly open and Two men Sitting in the Pulpit
Talking. one of them was Telling the other what
a Host of lives the Building of the Temple had
Cost How much Suffering and Sorrow, When
I Entered and Invited Them to Leave which
they Did. He was then Boarding at a Public
House North of the Temple across the street Kept
by a man By The Name of Slocom. After the
Temple was Burned He was Heard to Boast
That He saw the fire when it did not look
larger than a mans Hand, His Room was
facing the Temple The fire Started late at
Night when all were Supposed to be In bed
and asleep. Now add to this That the west
Basement window on The south side which
led to the Stairway Had been Taken out
And was sitting against the wall of the Building
Showing that no Key was used to Enter
the Building. And the fire was started in
the upper story. Now it is a Supposable
Case at least, That if a man saw the fire

There are some living now who can Coroberate
these Statements

In the spring of 1850 I again started westward
to follow my Kindred and Friends. on arriving
at Kanesville Iowa, I found some of them
there and Concluded to Stop there until another
Season And by the urgent Request of many
of my Friends I Commenced the practice of
of Medicine, this proved to be the great Cholera
year, and Consequently a Season of great distress
and Suffering and my Calls were So numerous
that for months I would get but little chance
to take off my Clothing to sleep this was also
a great year for Emegration to the mines. in
Colafornia, In the Spring of 1851 I Concluded
to follow my Brothers Joel & Benjamin to the
Rocky Mountains, ^(we started June 1st) But the waters of the Loup Fork,
And Elk Horn, were so High it was almost
Impossible to Cross them So it was Decided
to take a new Route that had not yet been
Explored to Cross the Head waters of these
Streams So on the 13th Day of June 1851 I
Started with my family and many others on
this unexplored journey and the Hardships
and Suffering we Endured was more than
I can Describe on paper, we travelled many
days ober a Sandy Desert almost without
food water or feed for Man or Beast But
after a Journey of Several weeks we arrived
at the Platte River, In Crossing the Bottom for
Several miles we passed through a Herd of
Buffalo which Extended as far as the Eye could
Reach Each way. and as we traveled on they
Parted Right and Left to let us pass through.

34

About Ten (10) Miles before we Reached the
Platte River, my son Milas Edgar was born
On the 31st Day of July. On that Night we Had
the Hardest Storm that I ever Remember in my
Life Thunder & Lightning, Wind and Rain, But
the sun shone Bright in the Morning. and
we Continued our Journey under more favroble
Circumstances the Rest of the way. we Reached
Salt Lake City about the 21st of October we
Remained in the City Several Days Visiting &c
and then Moved to Summit Creek utah to
Where my Brother, Benjamin was about to
Establish a Colony. Here I Built the First
Cabin. I Remained here a short time and
then Removed to Springville. where I Built
one of the first Houses on the City Lots. Here
I Remained Here I Remained until the
Indian Or Walker war Broke out and
Summit Creek was abandoned. I had Built
Several Houses which were all torn. Down
and we moved into the Fort. Here I was
Post Master, until the fall of 1853. where I
was Called to go and assist in Building
up Iron Co. & Learn the Piede language.
Where I went in the fall of 1853. Here in
Connection with my Nephew Nephi Johnson
we Compiled and Published the Piede Dialect.
and in the winter of 1853 I went to Salt
Lake City & got it Printed. and on our Return
we were Snow bound in the mountains and
Suffered much from Cold & Hunger being four
(4) Days without food. I Remained in Iron
Co about two years. The most of my time
among the Indians. and Exploring the mountains

I Remained in Iron Co about two years
And was then called back to Summit creek
to assist in Rebuilding that Place. This proved
to be a Grasshopper year. or year of Famine.
As I Raised Nothing through the Summer I
Concluded to Return back to Iron Co to Spend
the winter, and in the Spring I Returned to
Summit Creek (Now called Santaquin) Taking
with me Flour Enough to Last my Family
And Some others through the Famine.
During the Summer of 1857 I was appointed
Councilor to Bishop James S. Holman and ordained
a High Preist. under the Hands of Bishop
Blackburn at provo. I was also appointed
Clerk of The Branch and Post master which
Pasition I held until the Fall of 1859.
When I was Called to make a Settlement
at the Uinta Springs In Sanpete Co.
During The Summer I got the Land Surveyed
Laid out the Town of Fountaingreen and prepared
to Build up the place & Built the first Cabin
there. In the Fall Settlers began to come in
And I was appointed Bishop & also Post
Master. Everything went on well for a time.
But Domestic Difficulties arose and Part
of my Family Left me. And I then Returned
to Santaquin where I Remained until 1863
When I Removed to spring Lake where my
Brother Joseph Had Settled Here I again
Fitted up a Home for what Remained of my
Family. In the Spring of about 15th 1864 I started for
The Eastern Country Taking my oldest son
with me (Amos) our trip was Pleasant
and Rapid From Salt Lake to Council Bluffs

Nothing occuring of Interest until we Reached
the Crossing of the Platte River, Oposite Julesburg
There we Found the water High & the River
Overflowing its Banks and many Emigrants
waiting to cross. Here we met a Negro
with 13 yoke of oxen who offered to take us
over safely For six (10) Dollars For each wagon
This we Promised to pay Him and He Hitched
on to two wagons and started out The Cattle
Found bottom until they got within about
200 yards of the other Shore. Here they Struck
Swimming water & then The Leaders turned
Around and they all wound up like a Ball
And we Had a Lively Time Cutting them Loose
And never lost an Ox But we lay in the
water until after Dark Before we could get
The wagon out and then we Found we had
lost Everything Exept my Trunk and its Content
And one Set of Harness and a Buffalo Robe
But we soon Bought a few Supplies from
the Emegrants and in our way at ten o,clock
The next morning, The Rest of our Journey
was accomplished without anything occuring
worth Relating, we Had made the Journey
of 1,200 miles Inside of thirty (30) Days
From Home. At Council Bluff City I met
with a few of my old Friends and Acquintans
of 13 yrs ago and we Seemed glad to see me
and offered me many Kind nesses
we Remained Here about one month Fitting up
to Return Here I Bought Fitted up and
loaded three (3) of Teams with merchandise
for Utah and about the middle of July we
Started on our Return Trip Had Considerable

Bad Luck For a few Days Loosing Cattle Breaking
wagons &c But soon our Luck changed and we
got along without accident, we Had not traveled
Far before we began to Hear Rumours of Indian
Difficulties ahead and Soon Heard that the Sioux
Indians had Taken the warpath and were
Killing and Destroying all that come in their way
and we soon Began to meet the Ranchers coming
Into The settlements for safety and when we Reached
Fort Kearney we were Detained with all the
Emigration Six (6) weeks by the Troops at that
Place. About the first of September we were
Released & in company of about two Hundred
(200) wagons that had Gathered there we Continued
our Journey through Scenes of Desolation and
Destruction Ranches Destroyed Buildings Burned
People Murdered by the Indians and Every=
=thing abandoned To them and The wolves The
Last part of our Journey was through storms
and Snow we arrived in Salt Lake City
the 9th of November 1864 Having lost the most
of our stock leaving a part of our Loading
Along the Road and Suffering Everything but
Death when we arrived Home it was Completely
Worn out and Sick and Confined To my
bed Nearly all winter But Recovered the
usual Health in The Spring The Next Summer 1865
I was Called to Go South to assist in opening
up New sections of the Country and make
New Settlements I sold out my Property at
Spring Lake with the Intention of going South
In the Fall when the Company would start.
I sent all my Stock ahead by my Brother
and I moved to Spanish Fork to set up

and Remained there through the Summer, in
the Fall I fitted up Teams preparatory to Starting
and Returned to Spring Lake to finish fitting
up and wait for Company while there an accident
Happened to my family which hindered the till
in the winter So I concluded to wait till Spring
and go over to Fountaingreen to spend the Balance
of the winter where Some of my Children were
Living Here I Had a Anyland severe Spell
of Sickness which Lasted the most of the winter
and I was obliged to Sell one of my wagons
for Bread the winter was So Severe that Much
Stock Died of Starvation and amongst them
I Lost five (5) Head of Horses from my Team
and all of my Horned Stock but one Cow when
Spring came I found myself in very Poor
Health and in very poor Circumstances and
undecided what to do for a Team & food for
my family I finally Decided to get over
to Willow Creek in Juab co and try to get a
Team and go south as soon as I could I
Hired a man to Haul me over and got a
City lot and Commenced Building thinking
to Sell out for a Team But No such chance
occurred I Built a House Set out an orchard
and made what Improvements I was able
To There had just been a Town Surveyed and
Called Mona and my Improvements were about

And I then Comenced Keeping Boarders and Jotie
to making Trunks which I followed until 1883
when a Difficulty Broke out in my Domestic
Affairs which Terminated in all leaving me
for New Mexico Except my youngest Boy we
Remained at Mona until January 1884 to
Settle up Business and get Rid of the Post office
when we Took the Cars for Castle Valley where
Some of my Children were living, Here at
Huntington with the Help of my children we Build
a Cabbin and Prepared to try to make a living
and start anew as I had Done several times
before But I found That Hardships Exposure
and age Had Done their work and I
Had Nearly Done mine. My family did
not like New Mexico and Returned in 1885
two of my Children Stopping at Grand Valley
The Remainder came to me at Huntington Emery
Co. Utah. In the fall of 1886 with my Boy
Charley I went to Grand Valley to Spend the
Winter, we Had a very Pleasant visit with
The Children and in March we Returned To
Huntington where we Remained until November
1888 when I went to Manti to do some work
in the Temple for the Dead There on the 14th
Day of November, I was Married to Clarissa
Robertson By Daniel. H. Wells While over
There I went to foundangreen to visit my children

At Saint George called Jottings by the way
By Chas. E. Johnson Since my Health has failed
Me I have spend some time in Collecting and
Copying them in a Book and also Printing a
few more Pieces myself in pamphlet form
And also in Hunting out Genealogy in
Which I have accomplished a great work.
Much of my time for the Last four (4) years
has been Spent in this way, This is February
18th 1893 Should I live until Tomorrow my
years of Life will be Three Score and Ten.
<u>And Still able to do some good</u> —————

          In Looking over this Sketch I find I have
left out Several Incidents of my Life which
I will Here Jot Down
          During the summer of 1870 It was Thought
best to have a Reunion of the Johnson family
and an Invitation was Circulated throughout
the Territory for all to meet at Saint George
That Fall and Spend the winter at that
Place So about the first of October of that
year I fitted up two Teams and wagons
and Started Taking with me my wife and
family on our way we met with many old
friends and had a Very pleasant Journey
until we Reached Saint George
Here I met with four (4) Brothers and one
Sister and many more of our Kindred also
Brigham Young. George A Smith. And many
more of the Authorities of the Church who
Had gathered there to Spend the winter with
Us We had a Very pleasant time Visiting
with our Kindred and Friends During the
winter we Had a General Gathering in The

Saint George Hall. All of our Kindred and
many others were there Including Brigham Young,
George A Smith and others of the authorative,
with their wives Two Tables the Length of the
Hall were Loaded with the Choicest Food
After partaking of a Sumptuous Repast the
Rest of the Night was Spent in Dancing
and other amusements and we Had a time
long to be Remembered During the winter
we went to Kanab and to a little Stream
12 miles above which we Called Johnson
Here we made Arrangements For Colonizing
the Johnson Family But did not succeed in
Getting there On Returning to saint George
I found that two of my Horses had got
Drowned in a large Spring It was now
about time for our Returning to our North=
=ern Home So I fitted up one Team and we
were soon on our way we Had a Very pleasant
Journey Home and found Everything about as
we had left it

A Pateriarchal Blessing
Given under the Hands of John Smith Patriarch
upon the Head of George Washington Johnson Son
of Ezekiel and Julia Hills Johnson Born
February 19th 1823 Pomfret Chautauque Co N Y
    Brother George I lay my Hands upon
Thy Head in the name of the living God

Strength For many years until Thou shalt
Accomplish Every Purpose thy thy Heart desireth
That thy name may be Held in Honorable
Remembrance throughout all Generations thy
Posterity shall be as Numerous as the stars in
Heaven which Cannot be Numbered Thou shalt
be a Saviour upon Mount Zion and stand
with the Hundred and Forty Four Thousand
Clothed in White Thou shalt Have Power to
Go from land to land From sea to sea From
Island to Island And from Planet to Planet
And Visit the prisons where the spirits of thy
Departed Dwell Proclaiming Salvation through
all thy course with Mighty Power and Success
which Cannot now be Described thy Number
of thy Years shall be according to thy Faith
Even to see the Curtains of Zion Spread over
all the continent of America with all the
Beauty and Glory thereof. Thou shalt have
Thine Inheritance with thy Brethren in Time
and in Eternity and thy Posterity and
thy Children with thee possessing all the Riches
of Heaven and Earth To thy Full Satisfaction
If thou art faithfull Not one word shall
Fail For I seal it upon thee By the authority
of the priesthood And I seal Thee up to Eternal
Life. Amen. Given at Macedonia Hancock
County Illinois August 13 1844.

John Smith Patriarch

A Patriarchal Blessing
Given under the Hands of Willi[am]
Patriarch upon the Head of George [W]
Son of Ezekiel and Julia Hills J[ohnson]
Born February 19 1823 Pomfret C[o]
New York

Brother George In the [name of the]
Lord Jesus Christ I lay my Hand[s upon thy]
Head And by the authority of the [Priesthood]
I seal upon thee a Patriarchial Bl[essing]
I also Seal and Confirm upon th[ee]
Former Blessings and ordinations
and Expectations according to the orde[r]
for thy Lineage is in Israel thro[ugh]
of Ephraim and thou art an h[eir]
and Lineage To all the Blessings [given]
to Abram Isaac and Jacob an[d]
thee be thou faithfull to thy Desir[e]
Lord will not Leave thee Comfort[less]
give thee wife and Children to s[erve]
and give thee Health and Streng[th]
Everlasting Inheritence and by[?]
to the new and Everlasting Cove[nant]
Shalt be gathered with the Saint[s]
most High and with them Tak[e]
and Possess it Forever with all th[e]
Blessings pertaining thereto and
Stand upon thine Inheritence in t[he]
of the first Resurrection and be num[bered]
the faithfull For I seal these bl[essings]
in the name of Jesus amen
Given at Mona Juab Co Utah b[y]
William Mc B[rian]

., April 23 1893 Note
                    I Have just come into
Possescon of an old paper which goes back.
So far I thot I would insert a copy of it Here
in full as it Reaches back to my Boy hood day
and the most of it belongs to my family History
The words in Brackets I have Supplied

                    Kirtland apr 9th 1835 —
This Day a meeting was called at the House of
Lyman Sherman For the purpose of Blessing
His family with a Patriarchical Blessing after
The Company Had come together The Marriage
Ceremony of A. W. (Alexander white iples). and
E. S. (Esster Sherman) was Solomnised By Praye
by Wm E. McL (William E. McLelland) and The
Rites served by Esq Hanson after which the
Meeting Proceeded to Receive the Blessings under
the Hands of Pres J. S. sign (President Joseph
Smith sen) who commenced by Prayer.
     The Blessing Of Aseneth Sherman.
          Sist (er) Sherman Inasmuch as thou hast
been obedient to The Commandments Thou. hast.
Come out From the world In the name of J. C.
(Jesus christ) I bless thee with the Blessing
of thy progenitors and with a Fathers Blessing
and thou Shalt be Blest in thy old age and
thy Life is Sacred to thee For the lord Shall
keep it and shall Minister unto thee and then
Shall be gathered To thy Fathers in a good old
age and thy Children Shall call The Blessed
And I ask my Heavenly Father to Seal it Amen

upon thy Head in the Name of Jesus Christ
and Inasmuch as thou Hast no Father God shall
be thy Father and He shall comfort thee
and it Has been Promised too That thou
Shalt go forth and thy Lord Shall Minister
to (Thee) And thou shalt have power To command
The Waters and thou shalt Cause The Earth to
Tremble for thou art one of The Horns of
Joseph to Push the people Togather. and in
the name of Je(sus) I pronounce these Bless=
=ings upon thee and upon thy Children To the
latest Generation and I ask my Heavenly
Father To seal it Even so   Amen .

        Delena Sherman

Sister S(herman) I lay my Hands upon thy
Head in the Name(of Jesus) to Bless thee
And thou Shalt Receive a Blessing with thy
Husband And the Lord Shall Bless thee So thy
Heart shall be Drawn after the good of souls
So then Shall be with thy Husband Shall
yc Declare the things of The Kingdom and
He shall Return yea many times Shall He
Return and at the End of His Labors He shall
Return and you shall be Blest togather and
thy Soul Shall be Blessed with all the Blessings
of Heaven Inasmuch as thou Shalt ask in
Righeousness. And these things I Promise
to thee and ask my Heavenly Father To seal

And I say unto thee keep the Commandments
of God For Satan Shall seek to Destroy thee.
But He Shall not over come, in as much as thou
art faithfull and thou Shalt be Blessed with
Long Life Even until thou art Satisfied therewith
Thy name is written in Heaven Never more to
be Blotted out if faithfull and in the End of
thy Days thou Shalt be gathered Home to thy
Fathers and I ask my Heavenly Father to
Seal these Even So Amen

Almera Johnson

Sister (Almera) I Pronounce upon thy Head
The Blessing of a Father thou Hast had
much affliction because of thy Father and thou
Shalt be Delivered from that curse and Receive
the Blessings through the Pr't (Priesthood) of
M (Melchesedec) and now thou be Blest of
The Lord and yea thou art Blest of thy (Lord)
And if thou art faithfull thou Shalt come off
Conqueror, and thou Shalt be saved when
The Lord Shall (Come) and these Blessings with
all thy Heart can Desire In Righteousness art
Shine Even so Amen.

Susan Johnsons Blessing

S(ister Susan) I lay my Hands upon thy Head
And I say in His Name (the Lord) Lift up thy Head
And Rejoice for the Lord has seen thine afflic=
=tions in the Days of thy youth Because thou
Hast sought to Keep His Commandments and

His, and these Blessings I give you in the name
of J(esus) C(hrist) and thou shalt Receive a
Crown of Righteousness Even so Amen
The Blessing of Mary Johnson
I Lay my Hands in the Name of J C (Jesus
Christ) Thou shall be Blest of the Lord for thy
Father Hast also Sought to Destroy thy Peace
Because thou Hast been mindfull of the Lord
and thou Hast been Deprived of the Same But
the Lord shall Comfort thee and satan shall not
overcome Angels shall Minister unto thee, if
thou shalt seek it with thy Heart thy Tongue
Shall be Loosed and thy name is written
in Heaven. and I ask the Lord to Seal it
there and thou shalt be Blest with Heavens
Blessings Even so Amen
Marlow Everts
I Lay (my) Hands (upon thee) I Pronounce
Even the Blessing of A I J (Abraham Isaac
and Jacob) and Blessing shall C(ome) upon
thy Head (and the Head of thy seed If thou
shalt Have any) and the time shall Come
When thou shalt be Called to Declare the word
of god and if thou shalt be Faithfull thou
Shalt be Blest with the Blessings of Heaven
and in the Name of J C (Jesus Christ) I
Seal these Blessings upon thee and thy Pos=
=terity Even So Amen
Benjamin Johnson
Benjamin I Lay my Hands upon thee for thou
Hast a Right to it and I Bless thee with the
Blessing of a Father Inasmuch as thou shalt obey
the Covenants of the Lord and thou shalt Receive
the Mission which thy Brother (Seth) Has been

taken From, and if Faithfull thou shalt be
Crowned with Many Shevues and thou must
Prepare thy Heart and yo Forth into the watus
of Baptism and then shall Receive The Blessing
of Heaven and at last be Crowned in The Celestial
Kingdom Amen
   Joseph Johnson   Aprl 7" 1835
If thou will Listen to The Voice of
See The Lord and thou wilt follow thy Redeemer
into the waters of Baptism thou shalt be Blest
with The Blessing of a Father and Peradventure
the Lord will Give thy Father, and I ask my
Heavenly Father To Seal thee His, and I Seal
these Blessings upon thee in The name of J C
(Jesus Christ) Even so Amen Aprl 16
  The Blessing of Elder John Carrol 1835
Brother C(arrol) I Lay My Hands and Confirm
a Fathers Blessing the Lord Has Looked upon Thee
and He will be thy Father and the Lord will
throw arround Thee The arms of omnipoistence and
protect Thee For thou art a Chosen Vessel of the
Lord and thy words Shall peirce to The Heart of
Thine inemies For thy Name is written in Heaven
and Thou Shall Soar above the grave and all
Temporal Things and these things I Seal upon
thy Head in thy Name of thy Lord and thy
wife Shall be Blest in common with thee as I
Cannot See Her, and it Shall Comfort Her Heart
and these Blessings are to be to thy Children
to thy Latest generation Even so in the name
of The Lord Amen and Amen Augst 7" 1835
  The Blessing of Almon Sherman
Thou Hast not opened thy mouth as thou ought
to have Done But if thou wilt Humble thyself

Thou shalt be Blest with a Fathers Blessing for
the Lord has tried thee and thy Desires mostley
Have been pure and the Lord shall Bless thee and
He shall be Thy Father and thy Sorrows shall
be soosed and thou shall be Blest with many
Sheaves and thou shalt Lead many to Zion
And they Shall Call the Blessed and thou shalt
be Blest with all things which thou Conets
in Righteousness Desire And thou Shall go forth
and none Shall have Power to Stop thy Ministry
Nor take thy Life until thou shalt Lay it
Down for the cause of Christ and in the Name
Of the Lord these are yours if you seek them
with all thy Heart Even so Amen

In my Researches in geneology I have
accompesheed a great work in traceing out
The Dutton and De Graw families all Traces
of which had been lost for over 50 years All work had been
Done for the Dead of those families that
could be Done until I commenced a Research
And I have found about two Hundred more to work
for and on the 30th Day of June 1893 we
Starting for thy Manti Temple where we
Met others of the Kindred amounting in all
to 22 and we accompeshes the work for
about 50 of that Number I was Quite
Sick the most of the time But we had a

went to Soulainyreen and Spent two or Three Very Pleasant Days with my Children We then Returned Home feeling that our time had been well Spent and the Lord Had Prospered us in our work We arrived Home on the 22nd day of July 1893 Since then to the present time Nov 94 I have Spent the most of my Time in writing

I have Rec'd Three Patriarchal Blessings at Different Periods of Life under the Hands of Different Patriarchs of the church. One under the Hands of Joseph Smith sen the First Patriarch of the church a Copy of this I never Received The others are copied in this Book.

In the Fall of 1894 My health was very poor and I concluded to go to grand valley for the winter. I arrived there about the last of November and Remained with my children through the winter and when spring 1895 come they advised me to Remain which I concluded to do: and they Built me a very comfortable cabin for my use which I have occupied since on the Lot belonging to my Son B & D. A. Johnson

To be present at the Jubilee While
there I met many Old Friends, of years
gone Bye. Among them was my only
Brother living and several of my children
that I had not seen for many years
and I had a good visit with them
and Returned Home about the Last of
the month pretty well tired out and needing Rest. For the next two years there
was nothing much of Interest to Record
My health was quite poor so I could
not work much. and my sight and
Hearing was failing me fast and also
my Memory was getting very bad so I
found it quite difficult to properly
answer the few corespondents I had.
    On the Evening of the 18th of February,
1899 I Recieved from the Post Office an
Autograph Album. And when I opened it
and found the Names and good wishes
of One Branch of My Family numbering
about 80 members I could not have Recieved
a more pleasant surprise. nor a more
valued gift. The 19th (My 76 Birthday) past
off with a gathering of all my children
present. and all appeared to enjoy themselves. & were quite amused over the Album
which had been sent as a Birthday Gift.
This little Memento created in me an
Earnest desire to once more see all
my family. eer I past away. and
realizing that I could not live long
as I was getting old. & my health
being so poor.

Soon after this—sometime in March-99
—— ." My son - Joseph. E. came in from
Emery co= on business & remained a few
days visiting. & had Hitched his team ready
for returning, While He & my son—
David. A. were leaning over the Buggy
Wheel talking of the Parting, One said
unto the other— "How nice it would
be to have a Reunion of the family
& have all together once more" the other
Answered— Why Not? The Idea come
like Inspiration, & the parties were so
impressed, that they concluded to try
an Effort in that direction, While
Standing there talking. A committee
was Appointed to Arrange for the gathering
The result was— Joseph E. unhitched
his team, stayed another Evening, &
the Relatives were called together to
ratify the previous business of the
Brothers, Which was done The Committee appointed were —
    A. Johnson of Huntington Utah
    J. H. Johnson of Moab   "
    Steven Jones of Provo   "
The committee was notified of their ap-
pointment, When a correspondence began
as to time & place. to hold the Reunion
Huntington being central located, &
having some other advantages It was
decided to hold it there on the 1st
& 2nd of Sept 1899, The next in mos
business was to arrange a Program
After some correspondence Chairman

A.P. Johnson Blocked out and sent a coppy of a program to the other Members of the Committee for their approval. This was Agreeably done, & the Labor to prepare began in earnest for the Event. Reporters notes follows.

The 6 Months soon passed, & the time drew near. The first of the Relatives to reach this Point, was a Daughter Nancy. L. Woodward of Willow Creek Galatin Co = Montana. Who for 21 years had not been seen by but few of the relatives. & none had seen her for 14 years, untill her Arrival here on Aug 21st 1899. The intense feeling occasioned by this Meeting can only be realized by those who have experienced a similar one. Two pleasant days were spent visiting with her before any others arrived.

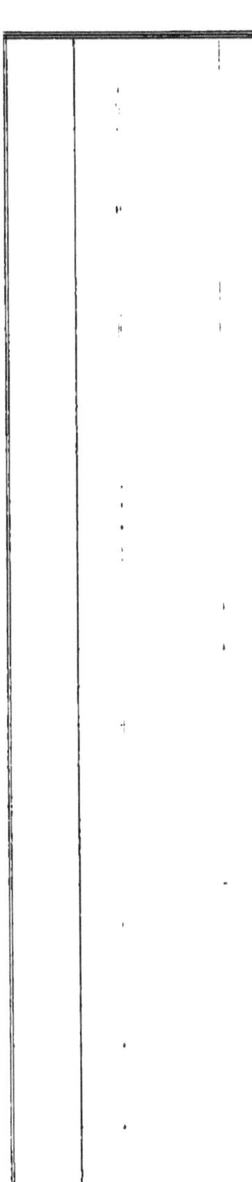

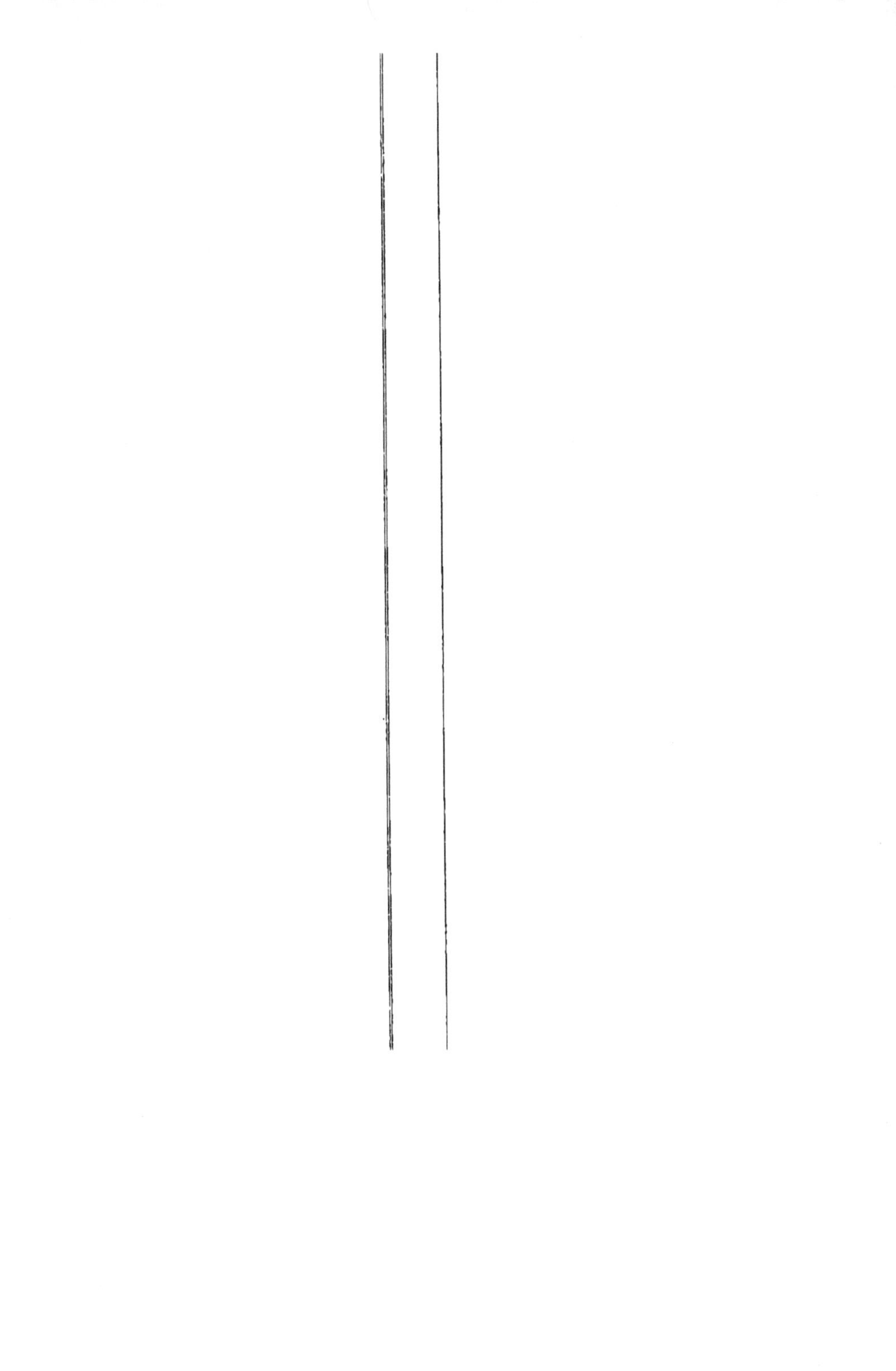

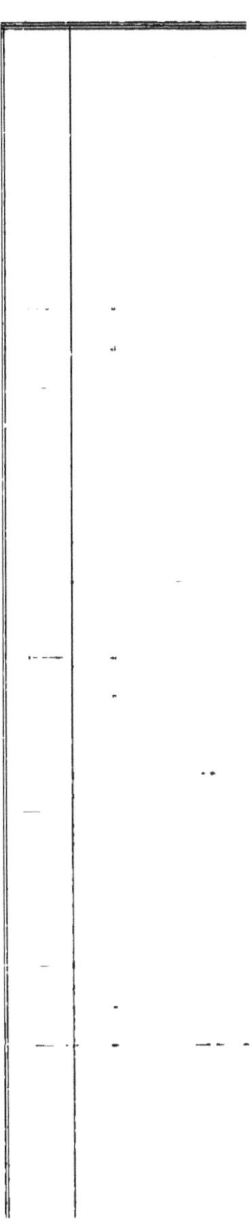

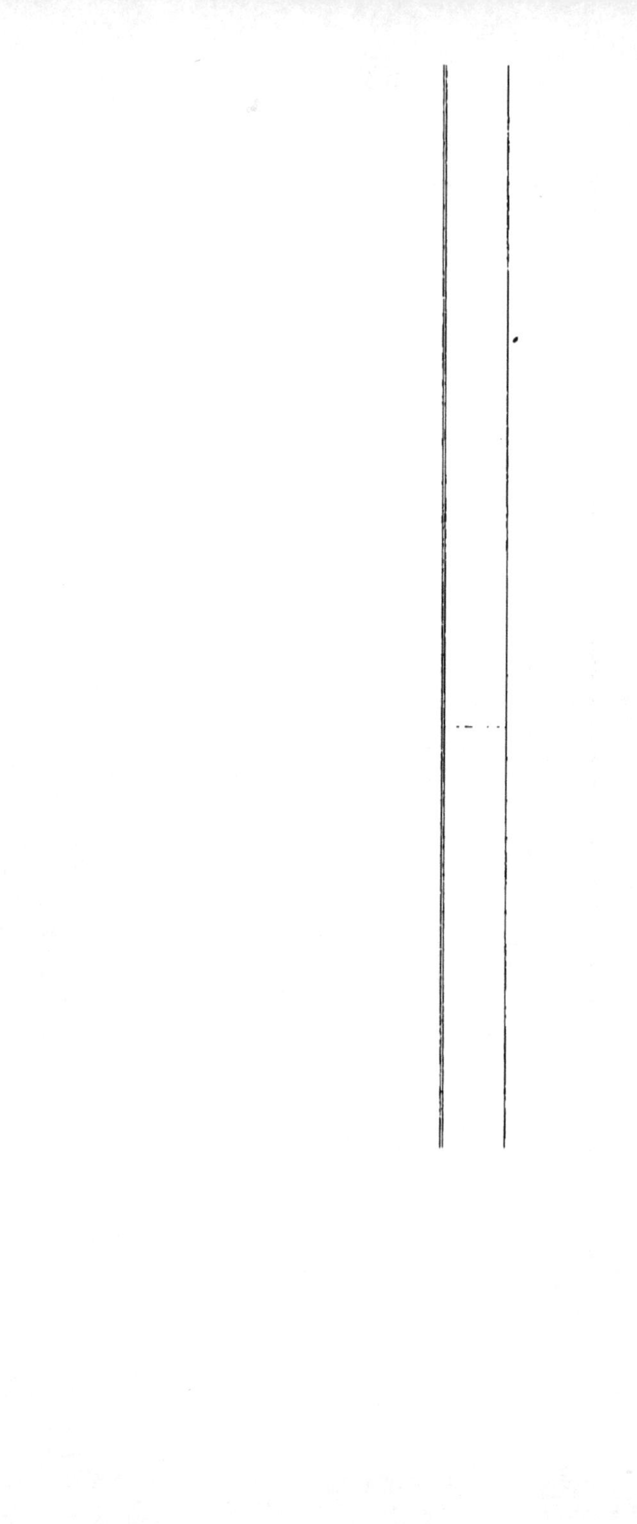

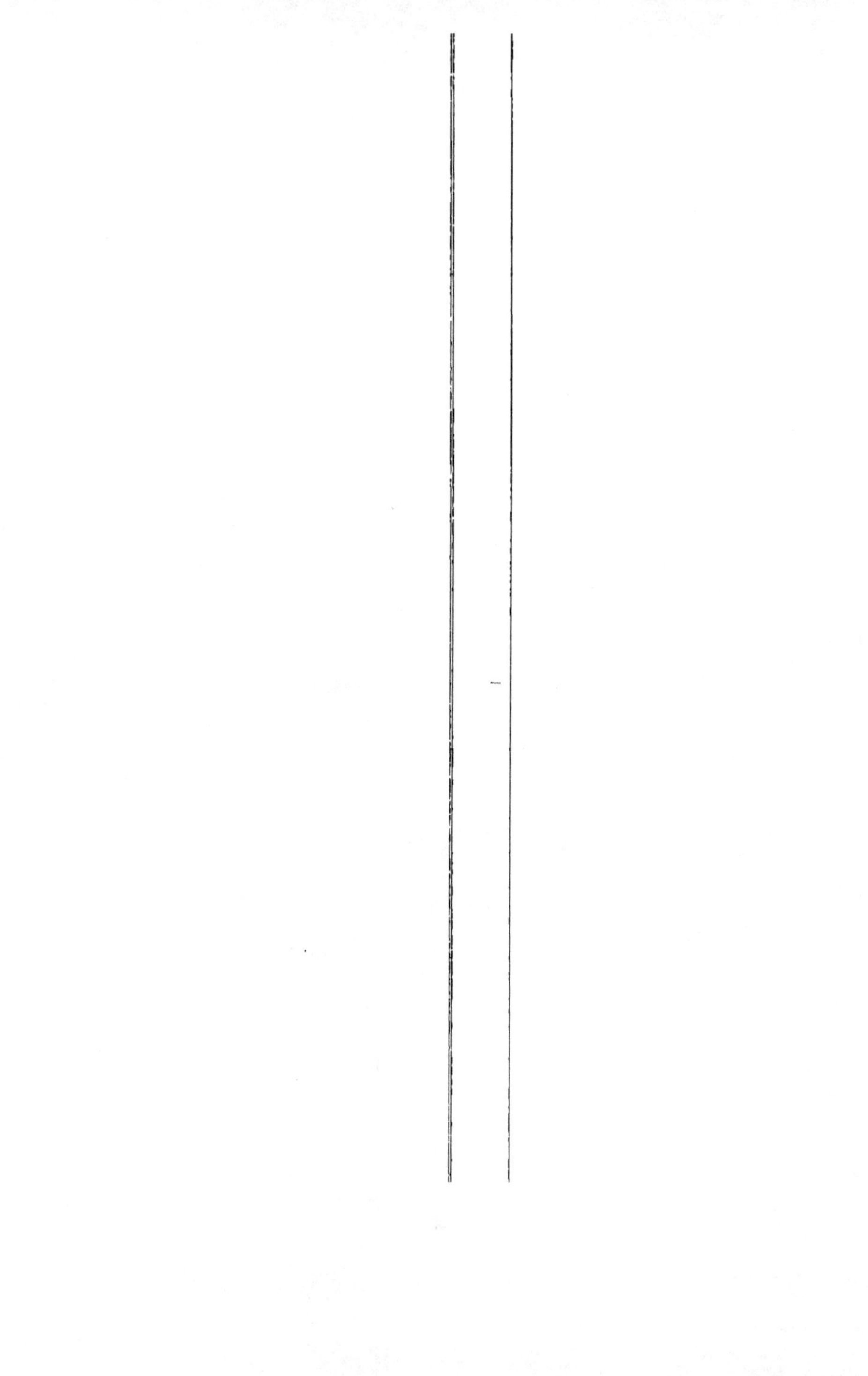

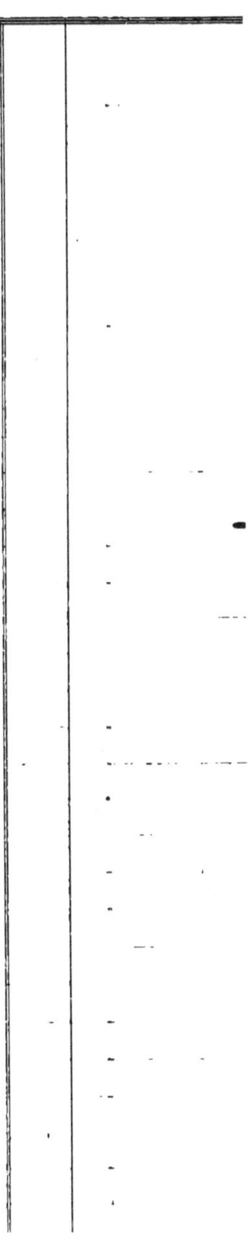

Kind Reader Perhaps you're Expecting to find
On these Pages a something to just suit your mind.
Some Sparklings of wit or some scraps of Satire
Or Perhaps Love or Romance your Thoughts would Inspire
Or should you to something more serious inclined
A Historical Sketch or Religeon Divine
Or whatever subject your Fancy may Choose
You may find if these Pages you Chance to peruse
But you're Likely to say at the End He's no Poet
So I'll tell you beforehand I very well know it
So pass your Opinion whatever it be
But you never could make a good Poet of me

My Mother

How oft fond memory Paints the scenes
  Of Times long Past away
When with thee Mother I did Dwell
  In Lands Far Far away
But Now thine Eye is closed by Death
  Yet unto thee is given
Immortal Sights to gaze upon
  The Brightness Een of Heaven
Now Neath the shades that thou didst love
  At Eve I love to sit
While Memories of other Times
  Around my Fancy Flit
I think upon the Household band
  That was Thy Hearts Delight
The Kind the Fair the loved the lost
  O! where are they Tonight
Ah Mother Thou Didst surely weep
  One lovely Summers Day
When I went from thy Humble Cot
  To Dwell in Lands away

Thy Tears did mingle then with mine
    We said the sad adieu
Ah little did I then believe
    I'd meet no more with you
Yes Mother when a stripling Boy
    I thought I loved thee well
But Oh I never knew Thy worth
    Till Forced to say Farewell
The years sped on and one by one
    The links fell from our Chain
The clasp was gone when Mother Died
    I will Ne,er be linked again
But since with us Thou couldst not stay
    Thy spirit would be Free
we'll strive to Emulate thy worth
    I've long to meet with thee

To My Wife

I am leaving thee in Sorrow
I am leaving thee in Tears
The Time Seems long to Thee love
    Tis only Months Not years
Tis Better thus to part love
    Than linger Here in pain
And Sigh for Better Days love
    That will not come again
I'm leaving Thee But weep not
    I'le soon come back to thee
And Bring The Hope and Comfort
    For then art Dear to me
I am Thinking of the past love
    Thy locks were Bright as gold
Thy Smile was soft But now love
    Our Hearts are Growing old

1864 1864

Tis not the Blossom faded
    From off thy cheek so fair
But winter comes too soon love
    And chilled the flowers there
Im leaving thee in sorrow
    Tis hard for us to part
But I will soon Return love
    Then Joy will fill thy Heart
Im leaving thee But weep not
    For when Ive crossed the plains
Ill Bring thee Joy and comfort
    When I Return again
Im leaving thee in sorrow
    But weep not thou for me
For God will speed my Journey
    Till I Return to thee

        To my Wife. No:
We are growing old togather
    You and I my Darling wife
We have Passed our sunny childhood
    We have Passed our Prime of life
Many Times the way weve traveled
    Has been wet with Bitter Tears
And weve Had our share of sorrow
    Through these long and weary years.
But weve oft met Rays of Sunshine
    Sheding light uppon our way
Bringing to us Joy and Pleasure
    As it Chaced the gloom away
But weve Passing Down Togather
    Down the Rugged Hill of life
And we soon shall Reach the Vallee
    That will End our Toil and strife

Yes Mother I've Come Back again
    In this once sacred place
I've traveled over Hill and Plain
    Since last I Saw thy face
And many weary years is past
    On fickle Fortunes track
But Here I am again at last
    Yes Mother I've Come back

Twas Here I left you Mother Dear
    And weeping Sisters Too
My Brothers too I left them here
    And friends both tried and true
But where are all those loved ones gone
    My Heart is fit to Break
For Here I am alone alone
    Yes Mother I've come back

But Mother lies on yonders Hill
    A Sister By Her side
And Friends of yore I loved so well.
    Have sickened too and Died
And some have gone to Distant lands
    To follow Fortunes Track
And Here I am alone alone
    Yes Mother I've come back

In this much Crowded Street
Amongst the Thousands that I See
Not one Known Face I met
Old Memories Crowd upon my Brain
Old Times are Coming back
Yes Mother I've come back

The Vales of Deseret   1864 While Traveling East

Oh I know a little Cottage Standing by a little Hill
With an orchard all arround it and near by a murmuring Rill
And inside that little Cottage There are Friends I neer Forget
But tis Friends among the Mountains In the Vales of Deseret

There the partner of my bosom and The Sharer of my Lot
And our Rosy little Children all Reside within the Cot
But theres Many a mile Between us and full many a sun will set
Ere I See the little ones, in The Vales of Deseret

I have traveled ober Mountains Ever Capped with Christal Snow
And beheld the mighty Desert as I cast my Eyes below
I have crossed the swelling Rivers and there many Hardships met
Since I left the little Cottage In The Vales of Deseret

But my Face I'll now turn Homeward To those loving Friends of yore
Torments wars and dire commotions all the land is Running oer
Then Oh what a Happy meeting when we all ayain leave met
In that little Humble Cottage in The Vales of Deseret

To my Sister Esther   Feb 19   1874

From Early Dawn till Dark at Night
So I will write a line to you
Tho: I can think of Nothing New
So lately Did I write before
That I can think of Nothing more
Unless the Whooping Cough we've Got
I cannot tell if tis or not
Poor Minnie Coughs both Night and Day
And Nothing Drives the Cough away
The others Cough but not so bad
And Eveline the Cough Has Had
The Baby worried so last Night
I got no sleep till Broad Day Light
To day My Head aches so severe
I Scarcely Know if I am Here
The Spring has been so cold and late
But Little Garden I can make
The Swelling Buds upon the Trees
Are opening out through Storm and Freeze
The grass is Green upon the Plain
And Flowers are Blooming out again
These all Proclaim that Spring has come
Though Fingers will get cold and numb
The Times Some better seem to be
A Dollar now and then I see
Though not Enough to keep me clear
of Daily wants and clothes to wear
I not a word from J E get
Or any of the Little Set
B J wrote to me from Spring Lake
He thinks as his Heart Nothing make
The D Ts are at Home Ere this
If Nothing with them went amiss
Tis Monday and the Finest Day

We've Had this Spring I'll Truely Say
So to the Garden I must Go
To plant the Seed and Plow and sow
To clean the House the women say
They must begin this very Day
So I must Plaster Fit the floor
And do a thousand things or more
At night I'm Tired as any Dog
And Tumble in just like a Hog
So I must bid you now good Day
For I have Nothing more to say
May Heavenly Blessings Ever be
With you to Keep you Company

A Burlesque

They Say John C Bennett is forever undone   1844
He Has Finished his course & his Race he has Run
He has Barked his Last Bark He has Told his Last Lie
And He soon to the Bottomless Regions will He's
                                    Crying. Oh Dear
For when He is Dead the young Devils will Come
And Shoulder his body and take it along
Saying while on the Earth sir you served us well
And Now I will Carry you Safely to Hell
                                    Crying Oh Dear
They will Take Him to Hell and when He gets there
Old Belzebub sits in his big Rocking Chair
Says Belzebub who have you got on your Back
Tis Bennett the Mormon Apostle Says Jack
                                    Crying Oh Dear
Says Belzebub Put him away in the Hole
And Bid the young Devils to fill it with Coal
And Put in the Brimstone and set it on fire
For sure there was Never before Such a Liar (Crying Oh Dear

To My Sister Esther (on the New order)

You may think it is Hard But I'll tell you the truth
I Believe as I did in The Days of my youth
When Joseph Preached to us the word of the Lord.
And told us The Kingdom of God was Restored
It Consisted the scum of the Poor of the Earth
No Matter what Station No matter what Birth
The meek and the lowly the Poor and down trod.
No Rich man could Enter the Kingdom of God
Far be it from me to say Brigham is wrong
Sincerely I've loved Him I have followed Him long
But still I must say He is only a man.
And Like all will make Money whenever He can
There is many a man would do Better No Doubt.
By Having His Distiny Here Pointed out
That man must lack some thing who ever He be
If I am that Person I yet Have to see
Although I am Poor and my living Not Good
And I often go short of good Clothing and Food
Yet Seasoned with Freedom a Crust would be Sweet
To Bondage and all you could lay at my Feet.
So now I conclude with these facts in Fall view
To not be in Haste in whatever I do
But Patiently wait till Its clear to my mind
And not be Like many who now go it Blind
When the gods Brot Religeon to Earth to Deal out
Our Family yet its Full Share without doubt
But some get too little and some yet a gorge
And Perhaps with the First is your Poor Brother gas,
Dont take it un kindly whatever you Do
Remember a Brother is Talking to you
With feelings of Kindness for friends who are Dear
And those who have left us and yet are so near
I think I have written Enough for today

On a Photograph

I know it looks not as it did
  When in her youthful prime
We stood before the alter and
  She placed her hand in mine
Bright was her eye and dark her hair
  And smooth her youthful brow
To love each other evermore
  We plighted there our vow
Since then full many a year has past
  And brought both joy and care
And left their furrows on the brow
  And frost upon the hair
But what care I for frosty hair
  Or furrows on the brow
The love I bore her on that day
  Is stronger, purer now

On a Photograph

It is not what it used to be
  There's frost upon the hair
The brow is farrowed o'er and time
  Has left the marks of care
But do not frown tho' fast years fall
  And lithe your form may be
For time will surely do for you
  What he has done for me

The friends I have cherished in life's early day
Side by side through this life we have toiled on for years
And shared with each other its joys and its tears
Until time in its flight has dropped snow on our heads
And left on our faces the traces of care
A few more short years and this life will be over
And we'll all meet again in a far brighter shore

To David

My thoughts have been wandering backwards
    Far back through the vista of years.
To a time when we should have been happy
    Ere we knew of dark sorrow and fears.
Of the boys and the girls our companions
    How well I remember them all
The spelling schools plays and rehearsals
    The singing schools parties and balls
How well I remember the school house
    Where Sheen kept the school by day
And at night us young fellows would gather
    With the girls for a dance or a play
There was manly a jolly good fellow
    And Daniel Sofence of the H. S.
And you and I made up the quorum
    That used to play cards with old top
There was Bill who would talk of his lasses
    Aurora Alunson and Prue
And Sanford and Sxen & Shuyler
    He treated you worse than a knave
There was many more boys I could mention
    But you will remember them all
And the jolly good times we we had with them
    At singing schools parties and balls

Then there was the girls Heaven Bless them
    The Mann spring of Every Joy
The Light Hearted Girls of our Boyhood
    Who would not again be a boy
I Know you Remember my Mary
    Lorana and Lydia and Nell
Pauline Eliza and Sarah
    And Ivanda who looked like a Doll
There was Dush who lived over the Hollow
    The School marm so gracefull and Joe
And many more Girls I could mention
    But you will Remember them all
Then there was old Lawson The Preacher
    Oh was, nt He Down on us Boys
He would Preach to us Hell and Damnation
    And tried to spoil all of our Joys
There was Gaylord the old Singing master
    Who Taught us Cold Hundred by note
And Kept in a Ayeing Shoe Leather
    And using His Awl Fast and Float
There was Morse who would play on his Fiddle
    And the young Folks would gather arround
What a Jolly good Time we Did Have then
    When we Dınced to that old Fiddles Sound
And His wife what a Jolly good woman
    Tho= Homely as Homely could be
The young Folks She Tried to make Happoy
    Such women we seldom now See
There was many more Jolly good Fellows
    And women true Hearted and Kind
But Ill not Stop to put them on paper
    Though their names are all fresh in my mind
But where are those Friends of our Boyhood
    How few of them now can be Found

One by one they are Passing away
But a few are still Scattered around
Manly Married got Rich and Respected
But Died in the East they say
But Daniel is somewhere in Utah
But where I am sure I dont know
But Sanford who Married my Mary
In Sanpete is Earning His Bread
And Curtis is in Calafornia
And Bill and Alanson are Dead
Of Schuyler and David I know not
Aurora is Roaming about
I cannot Tell where all The Rest are
The most of Them Dead without Doubt
And you and I still Cling together
But soon we must Follow the Rest
Where we'll meet no more Sorrow of trouble
In a far better Land of the Blest

Dixie   1870

The Time has now arrived For us to Haste away
As winter is approaching No longer we'll Delay
Lest storms upon the mountains should meet us on our way
As we go Down to Dixie
Our Friends have often urged us to Come to Dixies Land
Where milk and wine and Honey In Profusion are at Hand
And Every little luxury as plenty as the Sand
Way Down in sunny Dixie
We there shall meet our Friends and our Relatives So Dear
Our Brothers and our Sisters we have not seen for years
And have a social gathering with plenty of good chear
When we get Down to Dixie
They say tis very Healthy Way Down in Dixies Clime
The trees with Fruit are loaded and their grapes on Every Vine

The Rocks are full of Honey and theres gold in Every mine
                    Away Down in Sunny Dixie
But when the winters over Tis springtime of the year
And Flowers fill the Vales and Sun is shining Clear
We'll arise and Haste away to our Northern Homes So Dear
            Away From Sunny Dixie.

Darling Be True To me

Darling be true to me only be True
Cherish the Heart that is Faithfull to you
What care I tho' Friends be many or few
If you are True to me If you are True
Dark are the Clouds that Hang over me Now
Causing Deep wrinkles to furrow my Brow
Scattering Snow Flakes all over my Hair
Filling my bosom with Sorrow and care
Thou art the star of my Destiny Bright
Shedding its Rays my Dark Pathway to light
Leading me on through the Dark Sullen gloom
I have followed the on Till Dispair is my Doom
Fondly I've Cherished Thine Image for years
Tho' often thy Coldness has caused Bitter Tears
But the light of Thine Eye would chase Sorrow away
Bring Joy to my Heart with its lustrous Ray
Thine Image can Never be Lorn from my Heart
I must love thee still although Fickle thou art
My love is no pervything to change at my will
Altho' knowing thy Failing I must love thee Still
Return to me Darling be Constant once more
Ill love Thee as Fondly as Ever before
Be Blind to my Faults as to Thine I will be
A few days of Happiness still we may see
Our children will Bless us our friends will be true
To live For Each other we ar bound to do.

Be true to your Vows as it will be to mine
And be to Each other a True Valentine

God Bless our Home

Tis not Because Tis Beautifull
    This Cherished Home of ours
Tis But a Humble Cottage
    Amid the Trees and Flowers
But in this Humble Cot does Dwell
The Friends that I do love so well

Tis getting old and Moss Grown
    And falling to Decay
The Threshold and The Hearth Stone New
    Are wearing Fast away
By Foot steps that I love to Hear
Though not as light as once they were

Twas Many Many Years ago
    I Reared this Humble Cot
When not a Tree or Blade of grass
    Adorned the Barren spot
But now green grass and Trees abound
And Flowers Shed fragrence all around

I love that dear old Cottage
    Though Humble it may be
For many Happy Hours Ive spent
    With those so dear to me
In that old Cot among the Trees
Where Flowers Shed fragrence on the Breeze,

A Valentine

When Adam was created according to the plan
He stood within the Garden a solitary Man
God made a sleep come over Him & took from His side
And made of it a woman and gave Her for a Bride
To cheer His lonely pathway Down Life's uneven way
And make Him truly Happy and Bless Him Day by Day
Since then Has Every Adam been Seeking For a wife
In gentleness to guide him through all the Ills of Life
To share His joys and Sorrows to woman it is given
To be His only Polestar to guide him Here to Heaven
Gods Blessing on the woman as Maiden Mother wife
And Every True position She may assume in Life
And when we're called to leave it and try another Sphere
No matter where Her Home may be with Her may I it Share
A Home without a woman could be no Home for me
But Brightened by Her Presence Tis Home wherever it be
Except this little Ditty which I for thee Have Penned
And be to me most truly My wife my only Friend

My 54 Birth Day

Once more My Natal Day has come
   The Tally of my years
It Brings me Hopes of Happiness
   Though Frought with Doubts and Fears
The silvery Threads amongst my Hair
   My Brow well Farrowed o'er
Proclaim That I am growing old
   Ges I am fifty Four

I see my Children Women Men
   How strange it seems to me
It seems so short a Time Since I

The years are swiftly Passing Bye
    That will Return no more
They Tell me I am growing old
    Yes I am Fifty Four

The God of Nature

The God that others worship
    Is not the God For me
He is too Frail and Fickle
    He,s no Identity
But I,ve a God who Rules Supreme
In Natures works He may be seen
In His Majestic Beauty Oh Thats the God for me

He,s Not a god of anger
    He,s not a god of strife
He,s not a god Delighting
    In Taking Human Life
A god to Love but not to Fear
His works Proclaim it Every where
He watches over His Children Oh thats the god for me

I See Him in The Sunshine
    And in the opening flowers
I Hear Him in the Zephyrs
    That Murmurs through the Bowers
I feel His Presence Every where
His gentle voice His watchfull Care
Is ever Present with me Oh thats the God for me

He asks no Bend Submission
    To any Mortal Clan
In Kindness and in Reason
    He carries out His plan

No Priest or Rules to oppress
Or Rob us of what we Possess
In Love He Rules His Children Oh thats the God for me

I Love the Glorious Springtime
   That Brings Refreshing Showers
I Love the Fragrant Summer,
   With all its Buds and Flowers
I Love Fruit laden Autumn too
And Winter with its Frost and Snow
Gifts of the God of Nature Oh thats the God for me

Reverie

Oh how sad is my Heart and How lonely my Home
As Home from my Labor I silently come
Through Each Room as I wander my Footsteps Resound
On my Heart falls the Echo a sorrowfull sound
Oh sad is the Home where no Love can be Found
To scatter the Rays of Bright sunshine arround
With a kind word or look when we're weary & sad
From the Dear ones we Love How it makes the Heart glad
How Dreary the Home where Love always has Fled
And the germ of affection is withered and Dead
Where the Hearts we have Cherished from Boyhoods fond years
Is Dead to affection and Blind to our Tears
Oh Fashion and Pride Thou art cruel and Vain
How many Fond Hearts Thou Hast Severed in Twain
With thy tinsel and Charms and thy gordious array
With Deception and Vice thou art leading astray
May the Day Soon Return when thy Charm shall be Broke
And thy Victims No longer be Bound by thy yoke
When Pride and Deception with all their gay train
Will Decamp and old Truth Honest truth come and Reign

Happy Days of Yore

No matter what the world may say
  I cannot bid Her go
She's been a faithfull wife to me
  In days of long ago
Although on others She may smile
  And cares for me No more
Her smile was once as Bright for me
  In the Happy Days of Yore

Although she meets me with a Frown
  That Shadows o'er my Heart
Her Presence is Still Dear to me
  'Tis Hard 'tis Hard to part
Although Her actions plainly Tell
  My Happy Days are over
I never Never can Forget
  The Happy Days of Yore

I Cannot Leave My Children

I cannot Leave my Children
  They are all that's left to me
To cheer my lonely Pathway
  Oer life's Tempestuous Sea
For when this Life is near its End
  In them perhaps Ill find a Friend
I'd miss their Gentle Presence
  I miss their Boistrous Mirth
I'd miss their Noisy Footsteps
  Around my lonely Hearth
And when the Shades of Night appear
  On them I'd miss their Presence near.

To my Brother J. E. Johnson

Talk not to me of Pleasure Enjoyment or of Rest
With Friends I love So dearly and say Tis for t
To Leave all Cares behind me when Children must
And Each Day Brings the labor That gives Them Day

A week or two of Pleasure with Friends I love So
And Cares all left behind me and Plenty of go
Is Realy a Temptation Tis Hard to answer no
But Duty Bids me onward to labor foil and
How gladly would I treat you to wander oer
To pluck the mountain Flowers and watch the m
To angle in The streamlet to Hunt upon the pe
To climb The Mountain Gorges and Be a Boy ac
You Surely will Remember That Life is waning
And Each year as it passes Seems shorter than
That fortune Has been fickle in dealing out my sl
And Ever kept me Guarding the Grim wolf from
So I must still Keep toiling as year on year ge
But Hope it will be Bites in the Happy Huntin

Thoughts of the Past
I today in overhauling
    Picked up something on the Floor
Twas a Bundle of Old Letters
    Old and Time worn Nothing more
Dearest Husband Said The Letters
    Ah my Eyes are filled with Tears
Tis a sentence well Remembered
    Though not Heard for many years

Thoughts of years that long had Vain
    Chase Each other through my Mind

When to me Kind words were Spoken
    From a Heart so true and Kind
When Bright smiles were Shed around me
    Gentle words I then Did Hear
When around the Fireside gathered
    With our Friends and Children Dear

When with gentle smile she met me
    When my Daily toil was Oer
And our Children gathered Round us
    At our Humble Cottage Door
Now How changed Oh Draw the Curtain
    Let not words the Sequal tell
Social Happiness Has Vanished
    Lifes Enjoyment Fare you well

To My Brother Joel

Dear Brother in thinking oer Times that are Past
It seems to me years since I Heard from you Last
And I've almost forgotten your Present address
Of your Family matters I Realy Know Less
But I do not forget you are my Elder Brother
The senior of all of the Sons of our mother
Then why not be social with Brother and Friend
This life is but Short we are nearing the End
Then write me a letter and Let it be Long

With wife and five others I stick to the Sport
I have seventeen grand children all under ten
With Prospects all fair to make women and men
My Prospects in Business is not very Good
I have all I can do to get Clothing and ford
But I toil on in Hopes that the future may be
A little more Bright to my friends and to me
Then write to me often its pleasure to me
To Hear from my Friends wherso ever they be
May you many more years of true Happiness see
With peace yours Companion wherever you ae

To Laura

A few short months have Passed away
  Since she a youthfull Bride
Was standing by the altes
  And He was by Her side
Her Hopes were High for Happiness
  For many Many a year
With Him she loved with all Her Heart
  And friends she loved so Dear

How short the Time Then saw the change
  Shes laid Him in the Grave
And now she Mourns Her Dearest friend
  No Earthly Power Could save
Hard is Her lot though Bravely Bore
  But time will sooths the Pain
Though Clouds Eer shadow Dark as Night
  The sun will Shine again

Sir I'm Happy to Learn there is one in our Land
Who Has plenty of Money goods Houses and Lands
With Friends wifes and Children all Faithful and Kind
And Health of the Body and Peace of the mind
At Peace with all men and all good things in Store
What man on the earth Could be wishing for more
Then may you these Blessings Enjoy to a meet
Live many more years ere lifes Journey is over
May you lie Down in Peace when the Labour is won
When your husbend lifes work many you know is well Done
With me this worlds goods are but scanty indeed
Where I scew yet a Dollars a Hundred I need
To supply all my wants as Each Day Passes over
I must struggle to Keep the grim Wolf From my Door
As winter approaches my clothing is scant
No money to Buy the Provisions I want
To Provide for my wife and my Children and Friends
With Food and with Clothing my wants have no Ends

The Hollidays are Over

The Hollidays are ours the Brightest Days of all
The Lights are all Distinguished from Banquet and from Hall
Where dule the joyeous Dancers with wayward giddy feet
Are wheeling in the Waltzes to notes of music Sweet
And peels of joyous laughter Resounded through the Hall
And Happiness and Pleasure Presided over all.
Now all is Dark and Gloomy and silence Fills the Room
The Lights are all Extinguished and all in Sullen gloom
As Here I sit and Pondless I think of Days long Past
Of Days when I was Happy of Days too good to last
When was young bright dawled and Friends were kind and true
This world was Bright and joyous No sorrow then I Knew
Then like this Hall with Dancers my Heart was gay and light
Now Like this Hall Deserted Tis Sad and Dark as Night

My 56th Birth Day

How swiftly glide the Passing years
With all their Sorrows Joys and fears
That Bring me nearer to the Close
When I Shall find my last Repose
Another year Has flown away
And Brought again my Natal Day
With Wrinkled Brow and Frosty Hair
That Tell of Toil and anxious Care
My fifty Sixts year now is Past
And who shall Tell tis not the last
Of Toil and Sorrow pain and Woe
That I on Earth shall Have to Know
And when the Time shall Come may I
Be willing and Prepared to Die
And Have No fears that worse I'le find
When Earthley things are left behind

A Burlesque

Good Morning my friend Said the Devil one day
To a Tipper He met as He Past on His way
You seem to be Happy So Tell me I Pray
Has any one Started a Still up this way
For just as I Started Some one Did me Tell
That Somewhere in Meena a woman Did Dwell
Who Had gone into Business Such Liquor to Sell
So Poison Twould Kill all the Devils in Hell
And I thot I would just like to find out the Place
For to me it would be Such a lasting disgrace
For I never again Could old Belzebub Face
If to Such a Vile Haunt he my foot steps Should traile
I am fond of a Glass of good liquor you Know
And I often indulge with my friends down below
But to Such a Vile Haunt if I ever Should go

They would Drive me from Hell I would be stopping so low
There once was a woman From just such a place
Who come Down below From the Earth in disgrace
So Cold Belzebub Thought He would make a fyst quell
So He tried Her with Fire But she laughed in the Fall
Then we piled up The Brimstone and Built such a Fire
That we stood a mile off and we Dare not get nigher
But she laughed Him to Scorn with the flames Rising Higher
So she back to Earth came and we gained nothing By Her
Then Old Belzebub Feared She would come back again
And storm His Dominion with all His vile train
So He Placed a strong guard Round His Spacious Domain
And sent me to see if some news I could gain
We Have no place for such filthy wretches below
And in Heaven they will not admit them you know
Its Hard to tell where such vile wretches will go
But wherever it is She'll be filthy and low

Little, Merry, Mormons

We merry little Mormons are Joyables we have Come
To tell what we Intend to do when we are older grown
We are Resolved while we are young to study and to learn
To make good Honest truthfull wives when we that title earn
We are Resolved we will not wed a man that loves the glass
Or has a Habit of strong Drink do do we tell him Pass
We will not marry any man who smokes at chews the weed
His Habits would be Filthy & No no ser No Sir indeed
We will not marry any man who swears or is Profane
For in His word we are forbid to take His name in Vain
We will not marry any man who lounges in the street
For He would not a Home Provide or earn the Bread we eat
The man we marry must be pure in body and in mind
He must be Honest kind and true to sober thoughts inclined
He must be Free from every Sin that we have mentioned here

To such a man we'd give a Heart true Honest and Sincere
Though He might have a Dozen wives for that we would not care
We think we'd Done him just as well and of His love a could share
We'd Rather wed an honest man with all His Hearts he wives
Than any one who will indulge in all these little sins

To D, T, Le Baron

I have set myself Down for a want of a letter
On this Dirty Sheet of Paper to answer your letter,
For not writing before you Express to me sorrow
I Except your Excuse Now write sue Tomorrow.
The man that Called there To Williams was Sent
But it seems that He called upon you as He went
If the Bishop Dont Tithe your Long Green Down there
You may send it to me I'll Play Bishop out Here
You are Right when you fancy the face of the Bears
Through the long Dreary winter with poor Feed and horse clothes
Now I think at that Game Could we all once more play
As we did on my Fit it would Drive care away
But It's past we shall Never more meet again Here
When I think of the past in my Eye starts a Tear
There are left of our Early Companions but few
And we soon must Follow To earth but adieu
You say you are making a Fishing net now
I would Rather Have that one we had in Nauvoo
It would bring to my mind such a Crowd of old times
You will Think of them all Though they're not put in Rhyme
Yet I wish you Good luck with the one you will make
And I'll Help you in Eating the Fish you will Take
You say that the Boys are in School doing well
New this is The News I am glad you can tell
And I II pe you will send The Review out to me
For I am Quite anxious the Papers to see
The almanacks Come and was gladly Received

When the Baby was strong then you'd not have believed
You spoke of the fruit trees which you had to spare
No matter what kind I'll be glad of them here
And whatever you send to your credit I'll place
Tho your hearts are paid Till the last day of Grace
I'm Resolved on an orchard an orchard I'll have
Unless I should leave or be put in my Grave
To get some of good size I am somewhat inclined
And since I can Buy them that are true to their kind
And any good thing in the list of small Fruit
You of course will Remember Exactly will suit
As I cant do without food to Eat Clothe to wear
And for this I of course must begin to prepare
So I think that a Nursery Here would do well
So I think I will make one and Have trees to sell
All the sprouts from the orchard and seeds that will grow
In the spring I'll be glad of you surely will Know
And seeds for the garden I must have as well
For my own Private use & a few more to sell
For I have got nothing I Raised here last year
So just send me the price and the seeds you can spare
I must Turn Every Penny I can for my Bread
What I cant with my hands I must do with my head
I am sorry I have not of Plum stones a Peck
To make me a Hedge in my Garden out back
Of course you will laugh when you Read what I say
About setting out fruit trees at this late a day
But there is an old saying that will last forever
A thing thats Done late is better than Never
But Enough on this subject and too much by Half
So I'll quit it and give you a good chance to laugh
I think I have answered your letters all Right
So now I will say we are her all well to night
I have had a bad spell of that pain in my Head

And to day I have spent the most time in my bed
But I am better good say when you Keuel what I ncee
for I would not be scribbling Such nonsense to night
And this annoying cough two of the youngest have got
And they Keep us awake whether sleepy or not
And Eveline too is complaining to day
And who has not some aches I am sure I cant say
But I think we shall all soon gett better all Reyght
So Ill just take a snooze and Ill Bid you good m

To David Bowen

Tis Idle words to say weep not
  When Dearest Friends Depart
Although we Feel they are gone to Rest
  The Parting Rends the Heart
But when we Think a few short years
  And we shall meet again
To Live a Higher better Life
  And never part again
It soothes the anguish of the Heart
  And Helps the pangs to Bear
Although we sadly miss thee Here
  To Know we'll meet Thee there
Then may This Thought help you dear Friend
  Your Bitter grief to Bear
And soothe the anguish of your Heart
  To Know you'l meet Her there
I know she was your Dearest Friend
  True Loving faithfull Kind

Then courage take my Dearest Friend
  You soon will meet again
Where pain and sorrow never come
  To never part again

Who will Love me when I'm Old
Oh this world is sad and dreary
  As the years go slowly bye
Bringing to me every token
  That the End is drawing nigh.
Oft alone I sit and ponder
  Over this life so dark and cold
And the question oft arises
  Who will love me when I'm old.

Wrinkles deepen on my forehead
  Snow flakes gather on my hair
Sight grows dim and limbs grow shaky
  Sad result of age and care
I in youth had friends a plenty.
  Now their love is growing cold.
Who will care for me when feeble
  Who will love me when I'm old.

Had I one kind friend to cheer me
  On my sad and lonely way
With her presence ever near me.
  Turning darkness into day
Such a friend would be more precious
  To my Heart than gems or gold
She would cheer my lonely pathway
  She would love me when I'm old

Birth Day

Upon Your Natal Day Dear Friend
This Friendships Token I have Penned
Although Three Score and Ten are o,er
May you Enjoy another Score
With peace and Happiness and Health
And all that Constitutes true Wealth
And as Each Natal Day goes Round
With you may Every Joy abound
And Bring to mind Your absent Friend
This Token who to you have Penned.

Loneliness

Talk not to me of Loneliness when Friends are kind and true
Altho we are Called to Separate and Bid them all adieu
In when the time Shall Come to meet the Joy that fills Each Heart
Will more than pay the Hours of Grief Since we with them Did Part

But when the ones we Dearly Love Regardless of the pain
Departs and Leaves No Token that you'l Ever meet again
No Kindly look No pleasant word To soothe the aching Heart
But Coldly Leaves you without Hope Oh then Tis Hard to part

Tis then we feel a loneliness a Sinking at the Heart
An acheing Void we Cannot fill but must Endure the Smart
The Keenest pang the Heart can Know the most Enduring Pain
To give the love of all the Heart and not be loved again

My Dear Old Coat

Thou Dear old Coat with which I,ve passed
Through many a storm and wintry Blast
     I,ll Hang behind the Door
Cold winter, Past and Summer, near
With Cold I now Have Naught to fear

Thou Hast served me long and served me well
Thy worth Old Coat I cannot tell
        Thou wert my only Friend
With thee I've trod the Road of Life
Wraped in thee safe when storms were Rife
        On thee I could Depend
Thou art now much the worse of wear
With patches on thee Here and there
        With oft a Rent or spot
But these mischances fell on thee
In the good cause of serving me
        These marks of age thou'st got
Old Friend think not these marks of wear
Will cause me for thee Less to care
        Thou art no summer Friend
For thou art dearer far to me
Than Gaudy silk could Ever be
        On thee I could Depend
How Different those I own mean the while
The Sun of Fortune shines they'd smile
        But let a cloud appear
They're off like Shot thou art a warm
Kind Hearted friend in Every storm
        With thee I need not fear
Farewell old Friend but think thou not
That thou wilt Ever be forgot
        Through summers sultry Reign
When winter comes I'll come for you
And Have you Cleaned and mended too
        And put you on again
I'll Trust thy Friendship in these storm
For thou old friend will keep me warm
        Through winters storm & Rain

Like me thou art getting old and worn
By many a snag we Have been torn
        But we,l not part again

To E ---

When sickness and sorrow Encompass thee Round
And Social Companions No more can be found
And sorrow overshadows thy once loving Heart
There,s one who still Loves thee where.ever thou art

When Summer Friends Vanish thy charms shall Decay
And all thy Bright Prospects have faded away
When all Hope has Vanished and sad is thy Heart
There,s one who still Loves thee wherever thou art

When all your Bright Fancies allure you no more
And all your Past actions you stop to think over
There is one you will Pity if you have a Heart
For you,l know He Has Loved thee wherever thou a[rt]

Time surely will show you the Ruins you are der
And the Hearts you have wrecked in the Career you Pur.
God grant it may be Ere our Destiny Past
May you Love Him who Loved thee wherever thou art

      January 12th
I am thinking to day of the years that are Past
And Brot this day arround in Each year to the fus
With a thought of Remembrance By Each of our Race
Since So many Events on This Day we can truly

They also inform us a Sister was borne
And that our Father Died on this Day in the Morn.

One grandchild was Married on this Noted Day
And what more Has Happened I'm sure I cant say
In the years that are past we have oft met togather
And a good social time we have with Each other

But these times are all past we are passing away
And but few now Remain to Remember The Day
But as long as I live as this Day passes oer
I will Cherish Kind thoughts of those Dear friends of yore

My Mothers Ring

The gold was once my Fathers antique
    That made the little Band
Twas made and lettered to be worn
    Upon my Mothers Hand
But Ere she Saw the Precious Gem
    She went to Realms above
I Placed it on my finger then
    In Token of Her love

A Brother Saw the Precious gem
    And cruel words He Spake
I cast it From me Mothers Ring
    Our Friendship shall not Break
Let others wear the gem that will
    Thus no Charm for me
I'll wear no gem to Bring to mind
    The long She Bore for me

Spring (A Burlesque)

Ye Poets may muse on thy Beauties and sing
Of thy Buds and thy Flowers and thy Fragrance sweet spring
Thy beautifull sunshine the Dew on thy Flowers
The song thy Birds as they sing in thy Bowers
But what are such pleasures to me in my bed
Ceer shadowed with Beens & a pain in my Head
Each Joint in my body seems pulling apart
With not a Bright prospect to cheer a sad Heart
I must go to the office to see to the mail
Cer a package of seeds whm I keep them for sale
Then the cows are to milk and the pigs are to feed
And the wood is to chop I must put in the seed
From the Kitchen they call There's no flour or meat
No sugar tea coffee to Drink or to Eat
Not a Dime in the pocket and worried to death
Sick at Heart and in body can scarce draw a Breath
Then sing not of spring time unless it of Course.
Bring Health to my body and Dimes to my purse
And Peace of mind give me and Quiet Thats all
To enjoy Life in spring winter Summer or Fall

Spring

Spring is coming Bees are Humming in the fragrant air
Birds are singing Bells are Ringing all is Bright and fair
Flowers are Blooming all Perfuming Nature all is Bright
Sudrels Turning Bright Sun shining Shedding golden Light.

Shady Bowers Summer Flowers Scattered o'er the plain
Dew Drops glisten as we Listen to the Summer Rain
Singing Birds Lowing Herds Come with Beauteous Spring
Opening Flowers Summer Showers Summer months will Bring
Yellow Leaves golden sheaves in the Autumn Day
Winters Cold young and old Dance the time away

Home is still Home

Around my own Fireside I'm sitting tonight
The fire on the Hearth Burning cheerfull and Bright
No place on the Earth is so Pleasant to me
For home is still Home although Homely it be
Although I to a far Distant Country may Roam
My thoughts wander back to the Pleasures of Home
Then I sigh for the fireside so pleasant to me
For Home is still Home although Homely it be
Though Passion or Pleasure may charm me awhile
Or glittering gold may my moments beguile
Still the thought of that Fireside will still cling to me
For Home is still Home altho Homely it be
There is no place on Earth that to me is so Dear
As the Fireside my children are Clustering near
Then Tempt me not from it Tis Heaven to me
For Home is still Home although Homely it be
Altho poverty Drive me to leave it must go
A lingering look on Each loved one Bestow
With a prayer that Each loved one from Harm may be Free
For Home is still Home although Homely it be
My Home is a Cottage Surrounded by trees
Where Flowers Shed fragrance on Each swelling Breeze
Tis Old and fast going to Ruin like me
But Home is still Home although Homely it be

The Grumbler

Oh who can Immagyne what plague and what bothers
To try to write Verses to satisfy others
So Varied their Fancy No two can agree
What style or what subject good Verses Should be

For Instance The Matron wants Matters of Facts
Inclined to be Pious from scandall intact
While The Miss in Her teens must have Love and Romance
With Rambles by moonlight and meeting by chance

The Maiden of uncertain age Let me see
Mixt Equal Parts Gossip and Scandal and Tea
The Lady of Fashion Praise Beautifull face
She tone of a Bonnet Kings Diamonds & Lace

The Soldier of Skirmishes Battles and Slaughters
The Sailor of Dareing Deeds Done on the waters
The Bankes of Gold & the Brokes of Stocks
The Sportsman Fast Horses the tones of Kecks

The Gamester How Easy a fortune is made
The Merchant of Profit in Barter and trade
The Rumseller Mixing His Costumers Grog
Of Jolly good fellows As Drunk as a Hog

The Toper as Homeward He staggers along
If tis Vulgar Enough He is Singing Your song
While The Parson will say it all Very well
If it tells about Heaven and warns you from Hell

The Farmer green Meadows and Bright yellow grain
The Lady of Flowers Scattered oer the plain

The Doctor His Drugs & the Student His Books
Of The Swell you must Talks of His Exquisite Looks

Then How can we make up our Verses to suit
All grades from the Gentleman Down to the Brute
So I'll give up the problem & have no more Bother
But will Just suit my self have no care for another

Apple Blossoms

I gave to Her a Bunch of Flowers
    Of Virgin Apple Blossoms
One to adorn Her auburn Hair
    Another for Her Bosom
Says She How Sweet these Flowers are
    She placed one on Her bosom
The Other, in Her auburn Hair
    And Pinned them lest She'd loose them

Says I they are not Half so sweet
    As She who Does them wear
When she is loving Kind and true
    Says she Now do take care
These flowers are Beautiful to me
    When she for me will wear them
But when She Spurns them from my Hand
    I'll into Pieces tear them

Dollars and Dimes

I've been thinking to day of what absolute Sway
    In these Hard and unreasonable Times
Of so simple a thing as the Clear Penisant King
    Of the Powerfull Dollars and Dimes

No power so strong can compete with it long
  Against the Bright Ring and the chimes
It Holds a fall sway and will carry the Day
  The Ring of the Dollars and Dimes

If an office you crave it you surely can Have
  Although Hard for the poor are the times
If your Purse is Replete you can Never be Beat
  If you Shell out the Dollars and Dimes

At the Bar you appear and your case is Quite clear
  There are plenty will test to the chimes
That their Memory will Brighten that they can Enlighten
  The Jury For Dollars and Dimes

Though arrested and tried Ere The case they Decide
  You need Have no fear of the Times
You will surely get clear if your best friend is near
  The Powerfull Dollars and Dimes

Though in Prison you lie & are likely to Die
  No matter How great are your crimes
Though your Fate may be Sealed it may yet be appealed
  If you've Penty of Dollars and Dimes

But the want of The Ring of this powerfull thing
  Has sent good men to Prison sometimes
And there they may lie and languish and Die
  For want of these Dollars and Dimes

May the Day Come again when the powerfull Reign
  Of the Ring and the chink and the chimes
May be Shorn of its might and be used in the Right
  These Powerfull Dollars and Dimes

A Dollar or Two

Ye poets may sing of the power of dimes
And call their possession the greatest of crimes
But tell me without them what good you could do
I am sure I'd be glad of a Dollar or Two

In the Shop you see something you really admire
A present for wife you have long wished to Buy Her
You feel in your Pockets what more can you do
In Hopes you may there find a Dollar or Two

You go to the Restaurant for a Square meal
Your Stomach is Empty quite Hungry you feel
Your Pockets are Empty it makes you feel Blue
How then would you fancy a Dollar or two

You are sick and discouraged and likely to Die
You call in the Doctor as He passes By
You want His advice & His Medicine too
But He is in want of a Dollar or two

Your Lawyer will tell you your case is quite clear
He can soon set you Free you have Nothing to Fear
When He Pockets the fee He's Expecting from you
But you languish in Jail for a Dollar or two

Your wife will be asking for money to Buy
Some nice little thing She may have in Her eye
Your children want clothing But what can you do
If you are not possessed of a Dollar or two

For in this Hard world it pleasant to View
The Bright shining Face of a Dollar or two

All men seek to win it the Root of all Evil
It makes some a Heaven sends some to the Devil
Yet tis pleasant to Hear as we pas the world through
The Ring and the Chunk of a Dollar or two

Will They Miss Me

Will they miss me at Home will they miss me
When I am laid low on my Bed
Will they silently gather arround me
And shed on my Coffin a Tear
Will they miss me arround the Home fireside
When the Shadows of night over them creep
When the Children Retire to their Slumbers
Will they miss me to watch over their Sleep
When the Children Return to the Homestead
Will they miss me arround the long Hearth
When they think of the one that is absent
Will a Shadow come over their mirth
Will they think of the words I have spoken
And say He was always our Friend
And although He was Plain and outspoken
He loved us Each one to the End
Will they Kindly look over my actions
And say Though His Faults were not few
He never Intended to wrong us
His Heart was still loving and True
Will they say Though he never was Happy
He still loved His Children and wife
And True friends wherever He found them
So Him they were all in this life
Will they use all my Faults as a Beacon

To steadily Guide Their own Barque
And shun all the Rocks I Have wrecked on.
Though the way may be Stormy and Dark
It's Enough if they Know all my actions
Were Prompted for ultimate Good
And if I have Failed in my Purpose
I for them Have Done all that I Could

My Children

I have Watched o'er my Children for many long years
I have Toiled for their Comfort Through sorrow and Tears
I have watched by their cradle I've watched by their bed.
And over their slumbers Sad Tears I have shed

When Prostrate in sickness my children and wife
Have always been foremost with me in this life
Till my children have grown to be women and men
And left the old cottage where long they have been

They have wandered away and each Built a new cot.
And the old Ruined Homestead They all were forgot
And I have grown Feeble and wrinkled and grey
And weary of life I shall soon pass away.

But it matters not now as they need not my care
They have left me alone my sad Burden to bear
And the old Ruined cottage they seldom come near
To light by their presence the loneliness there.

They know not How sad is my Heart as I Roam
Around the old Cottage they once called their Home
Or How lonely to me when my Days work is Done
To Return to the Cottage Deserted and lone

I shall patiently wait For the time Drawith near
When I too shall Leave the old Cottage So Dear
All my Friends will then say It is all for the best
Death Has Freed Him from sorrow He's gone to His Rest

Fifty Years ago

I Dreamed I was a Boy again
    And By my Mothers Knee
I listened to the Fervant Prayer
    She offered up for me
Again I saw my childhood Home
    The place that Gave me Birth
With Friends and Kindred gathered Round
    The old Familier Hearth
The Bible lay upon the Stand
    Just as it used to do
When I was in my childhood Home
    Just Fifty years ago

The old Dutch Clock Hung on the wall
    The Cupbord too was there
The Pictures on the Mantlepiece
    And Mothers Old arm Chair
Again I wandered through the woods
    Where oft in Childhoods hours
I've wandered Forth to gather nuts
    Or cull the fragrant Flowers
I wandered oer the Meadows too
    Where Berries used to grow
Twas Just the same as when a Boy
    Just Fifty years ago

The Orchard too where oft I've sat
    To watch the Busy Bee

Just as they used to be
The Barn the Corn House and the Spring
  Where oft in summer day,
I've Knelt be side to get a Drink
  When Tired of Boyish Play
The Gulf Set where I Drove the Cows.
  As il to school did go
To Learn to Read my Alphabet
  Just Fifty years ago

Ah me that was a Happy Dream
  That Dream of childhoods Hours
When all the Thorns of life were gone
  And left the Brightest Flowers
But those Bright Days will no more come
  Whill I on Earth Remain
My Childhood Home my Early friends
  I'le Never See again
A few more years of Toil and Strife
  Ere I am Called to go
To meet those Friends I loved so well
  Just Fifty years ago

On the Plains (July 31st 1857)

I'm Twenty Eight years old He said
  What visions fill the mind
Of Travels on the Desert Plains,
  Tornadoes Storms and Wind
We Had travelled many weary Days
  Upon the Desert Plains
When For Refreshments we had stopped
  Our little pilgrim Train

A little stream went Ripling Bye
The grass arround was Green
It seemed to us the Brightest spot
For many Days we'd seen
But Hark the Rifle crack I hear
That lays the Bison low
And soon we Feast upon the Hump
Of the Fatal Buffalo

But now the sun Dellining West
Foretells we must be gone
But Hark I Hear a womans Moan
As we are left alone
An Hour goes Bye another Hour
And yet we Hear Remain
O Glorious News a child is Born
Upon the Desert plain

And once again we're on our way
To overtake the Rest
But Oh what Visions fill the Eye
Extending East and west
The Bison Gathered on the plains
In Millions what a sight
And as we Traveled on our way
They parted left and Right

Now as the Shades of night appears
Upon a Distant Flat
The cheerfull camp fires we beheld
Upon the River platte
With Joy again we meet our Friends
Around the camp fire Blaze

And late at night Retire to Rest
  To Dream of better days

But Oh that night the wind arose
  The Rain in Torrents fell
The Thunder Rooled the Lightning flashed
  More Fierce than words can tell
The Child and Mother with the Rest
  Were Drenched in every field
And yet He tries to Sell the Tale
  I'm Twenty Eight years old

Since then the years that's past have made
  Deep wrinkles in my Brow
My Hair is grey my sight is dim
  I seem an Old man now
But oft I think upon the Time
  The Story I have Told
When I was young and in my prime
  Just Twenty Eight years old

Good Bye

It is lonesome I know as I look through the town
With scarcely a Hoodlum or Bummer around
The whiskey Saloon is now labeled to let
On the steps of the Store there are few now to set
No Drunkards we see as we pass up the street
To swagger and Swear and insult all they meet
The Town is So Quiet it's lonesome you see
But this is the kind of a lonesome for me

The path over the Square up to where it once stood
Is growing to weeds it is seldom now trod

The old Whiskey Bummers stand round on the street
In Hopes to meet some one with whiskey to treat
They Have our good wishes that they Very soon
Will Follow their Idol the whiskey saloon
And leave us as lonesome as lonesome can be
For this is the kind of a lonesome for me

Now we Hope for the Day when our women can walk
On the street without Hearing Profane Vulgar talk.
Or being Insulted by Vile Drunken men
Who used to be seen at the low whiskey dem
It has gone from our Gaze like the Visions of night
If we Never again Should behold it all Right
If the topers all Follow It lonesome would be
But this is the kind of a lonesome for me

Fashion

Oh what a state the world is in
    And still is getting worse
With pride and Fashion Bearing Rule
    Societies Great curse
You meet a lady on the street
    Oh Dont she put on airs
It Took fifteen or Twenty yards
    To make the Dress She wears
Tis Trimmed with Ruffles Tuck and Frills
    With Riblonds and with lace
And over all She wears a Coat
    That any Swell would grace
The Jaunty Hat upon her Head
    With Flowers is laden Down
And underneath She wears a Braid
    That fills the Maxie Crown

And oh the jewels that she wears
    If gold would break a bank
You gaze upon her and you think
    A lady shure of rank
But list awhile and hear her talk
    You soon will change your mind
She to the lower class belongs
    You by her talk will read
She talks of Charley Pete or Ned
    At the saloon she's met
And of the jolly times she's had
    with all the jolly set
And as for modesty and grace
    The words are absolete
She'l laugh and gossip talk and jeer
    with Hoodlums on the street
And if a Husband she has got
    He's with the Beats no doubt
Where all such useless things should be
    He's Nothing but a lout
And only fit to stay at Home
    And see that all is right
And furnish money for Her purse
    And find the Beats at night
But if Her Husband in Desgust
    Has left and she is free
The Children go in dirt and Rags
    A wretched sight to see
She'l take a jaunt upon the cars
    To see the sights she'l say
And if she goes without Escort
    She'l find it on the way
She's Brass enough to introduce
    erself in any place

So Doctors Lawyers Judges all
  And thinks it no Disgrace
So Smilingly She talks of Moll
  And Pet names all Her Chums
But Dont She give Her Husband fits
  Whenever He near Her comes
Now if such women are allowed
  In good society
Good Honest wives will soon become
  A thing that used to be
The Picture is not over Drawn
  You.l See Her on the street
At the saloons at whiskey Dens
  Where Hoodlums often meet

To My Lady Friends

Dear Friends For the favor so kindly you.ve Rendered
In sending the Quilt Blocks I had asked of. Each one
I can do Nothing more when my thanks. I have tendered
To Repay you the favor so Kindly you.ve Done

When I Thought of The whims and determined to Try it
I very much feared that my Friends were but few
And I did not believe I would get Enough By it
To make up a Quilt with the best I could do

But soon they were coming one after another
until I Had more than was Needed for one
And still they were coming Now there was the Bother
There must be none left when the Quilt shall be Done

A Happy thought strikes me I.ll put them together
And make up another the best I can do

And when I shall See them Ill Ever Remember
I Had Plenty of Friends when I thought them so few

May god Bless you all who have thought of me Kindly
May Happiness Ever your Pathway attend
For the Token you,ve sent me will Ever Remind me
Of those who still claim the Dear Title of Friend.

The Old Dinner Horn

How well I Remember the Home of my Childhood
That Bright sunny Spot where I first Saw the Light
The Orchard the Meadow the Fields and the wild wood
No spot on the Earth Could to me be so Bright
How oft I have wandered over fields & oer Meadows
To gather the Flowers wet with Dew of the Morn
And list to the Song of the Lark and the Robin
Until Called to Return by the old Dinner Horn

How well I Remember Each Tree in the orchard
Each Shrub and Each Flower in the garden that grew
The well and the Spring and the Brick Yard near by it
And the Meadow Bedecked with the Bright morning Dew
And the Bees when they swarmed Oh what Dine and Clatter
To cause them to light on the old apple thorn
What Ringing of Bells and what Dashing of ....
And the sweetest of Music the old Dinner Horn

How well I Remember the path through the Gulf Lot
which oft I have followed in going to school
So Drive off the Cows and to leave them in pasture
until I was Released from the Rod and the Rule
To scatter the Hay I would go to the meadow
Or Ride on old Katy to plow out the Corn

Or pile up the Brush in the Clearing and Burn it
Till Id Hear the sweet sound of the old Dinner Horn

Since then I have listened to strains of sweet music
The sweetest that Nature or art could Produce
The song of the Birds The Harp Organ & Viol
The Sweetest of singing But then tis no use
To Compare with the Notes that I Heard in my childhood
On that Bright sunny Spot in the place I was born
Give me back the sweet strains of that Dear cherished Music
My Mother to Blow it the old Dinner Horn

The Signs of the Times (to JES)

Of the signs of the times I am thinking to night
And Im Prompted to Take up my Pencil and write
And as you in your letter Have Flattered my Muse
I'll Dedicate to you my thoughts if you choose
When I was a lad many long years ago
A Prophet and Seer lived near By us you know
Who told us the Time was then Nearly at Hand
When Death and Destruction should Visit the land
When Famine and Pestilence sorrow and Pain
Should Come to the Earth and Have absolute Reign
But the saints should be gathered away in the west
Where they Should be sheltered Protected and Best
Till the Night Should be Past and the Dawn should appear
That would open to us the Millennial year
The wise men now Tell us the the Time Has now come
When Earth is begining to meet Her sad Doom
The Plague is now Raging in the East and the North
And thousands on thousands are Swept from the Earth
And Famine and Pestilence Stalk through the land
And War and Destruction are nearly at Hand

That the Next Seven Years Dire Destruction shall Reign
Then Joy will Revisit the Earth once again
But They say that the Land we Inherit shall be
from Death and Destruction by far the most free
Now there is an old Book that we all used to Read
And our Mother oft taught us its Precepts to Heed
In that Book we are told that there would be a Time
When the Earth would be Cleansed from Corruption & crime
That the Saints to the Tops of the mountains would flee
Where for a time from the Scourge would be Free
That War and Commotion would Stalk through the Land
And Famine and Pestilence Go Hand in Hand
Till the Wicked were slain and the Earth became Pure
Then the Saints would go forth and Enjoy it once more
Now the prophet He told us god sent Him to Preach
And to this Generation these Principles Teach
By Science the wise men Have Learned what they know
On the Map of the Heavens it Plainly Doth Show
The Book Gives traditions Some thousands years old
All tell the same Tale as plain as can be told
Now what Shall we Think is it Really the Case
That we all these Scourges must meet face to face
That the prophets of old and the one of our Youth
And the wise men have all of them told us The Truth
Then we Surely must all be prepared for the worst
For the Earth by some power has been surely accursed
Then the best we can do is to stay where we are
And for all these Scourges ourselves to Prepare

Six Little Graves

Six little graves Lay side By side
All from one Mothers fold
In one short month they all had Died
And laid Beneath the mould

How much of Grief a Heart may bear
    This mother well may know
By Deaths cold Icy Hand to lay
    Them in the Grave so low

There is a Hope for those who weep
    For Friends whose gone before
To meet them in a Brighter Land
    Where parting is no more
Where Death and sorrow Never come
    To mar our Happiness
Where Love and Peace and Joy abound
    In one Eternal Bliss

Then may This Hope Inspire your Heart
    And Help you Bear the pain
To Know the Loss to you so great
    To them is only Gain
And when your Earthly work is done
    And all your Trials Oer
You then will meet your Little ones
    Where Parting is no more

        Four Little Graves
I saw them Lay Him in His grave
    Three others By His Side
The Earth was Damp upon them all
    So lately they Had Died
The grief that wrung the parents Hearts
    No Human Tongue Can Tell
As Earth upon the Coffins lid
    In Solomn Measure Tell

The Fountains of the Heart were closed
    From Tears to your Relief
But Branch did they struggle with
    Their sad and Bitter Grief
Your Little Buds Have Drooped and Died
    Ere they were in their Bloom
To Blossom in a Brighter Land
    Where Death Can Never Come
This is the only Hope that we
    Can Cherish in our Grief
And if we truly Cherish it
    It will surely give Relief.

                A Valentine.
No Gaudy Tinseled Valentine
    Have I to Offer thee
Nor will I give the Honeyed words
    Of Foolish Flattery
Nor Talk of Cupids wiles and Darts
    As others often do
But Plainly Tell thee of the Love
    I ever Bear for You

Tis not a Childish Love to change
    With Every Fault I See
For when I see your Faults I know
    You Bear with Faults from me
Our Faults have caused me Sad Regrets
    And many Bitter Tears
But never makes my Love grow less
    It strengthens with my years

Some Love an angel Deer or Duck
    Such things I know are common

But such would News do for me
    I love you as a woman
To be thy Hope thy Joy the Light
    That shines within our Dwelling
Or Blight my Life and cause me pain
    And sorrow beyond Telling

Then may we over come Each word
    Or Action causing pain
And Try to live a better Life
    And Happy be again
And may Each Future year Increase
    Our Hope Our Joy Our Peace
And lessen Sorrow Toil and pain
    And Happiness Increase

My 57th Birth Day

How swiftly Do the years go Bye
    With all their Toil and care
And leave their Farrows on the Brow
    And Frost up on the Hair
Another year Has Flown away
    And I am Fifty Seven
I've one year less on Earth to Toil
    And one year Nearer Heaven

Mormon Creed

Oh How the Times have Changed since I was but a Boy at home
When Joseph used to Talk to us and Tell of things to come
He gave to us these good advice which we should always Heed
And treasure up within our Hearts Twas called the Mormon creed
        Twas Mind your Business ~~Electioneer~~
            With others never meddle
        Hear what you Hear in street or Hall
            Be sure you do not Peddle

He told of trials that we all were certain to endure
So Bring our Hearts to serve the Lord this Blessings to secure
He told us to be honest and true to sisters and to Brothers
And always give a Helping Hand to lift up one another
(Chorus)
The Times have altered much since then and Everything they Changed
The People go about the street as if they were Deranged
They gather News from house to house to Peddle in the Street
And always Have some Shocking news to tell to those they meet
        And other peoples Business Money
            With theirs they do not meddle
        And what they Hear in Street or Hall
            They Magnify and Peddle

They go about from house to house Defaming every Neighbor
Enlarging every fault instead of doing honest labor
They always Have some Precious news some more or less amusing
So Magnify and go about this dreadful news Retailing

They gather in some neighbors House and spend the livelong Day
To scandalize some Neighbor that Perchance may be away
They magnify each failing of each Sister & each Brother,
But never think it worth their while to lift up one another

Prologue

Dear Friends I am Happy to meet with you Here
To see your Bright Faces your Voices to Hear,
And to Know you are trying yourselves to prepare
To Carry the Burden you'l soon Have to bear

This Burden we Have Borne through the Heat of the Day
Till the years on our Heads Show we are passing away
When we Sit down to Rest on your shoulders twill fall
And the time will be short for the End draweth nigh

For your Kind thoughts of me I am thankfull indeed
You have asked me before you a Burlesque to Read
Then may you derive from it good in the End
For I would not be less to you all than a Friend

Burlesque

Oh come on my Boys to the steps of the store
We Have now a large crowd But there's still Room for more
We want to Enlist every one that we can
And we,l find you all something to do a a man

We want some to whittle the steps of the store
And stare at each woman that passes the Door
And make Slight Remarks as she goes in & out
And what Does not concern them to try to find out

Then out on the street we Shall want a few more
To Stand around Idly in front of the store

And watch Every person that goes up or Down
And find out the Business of all in the town

Then we want a few more around to Each House to go
And tell Everything they Can guess at or Know
Concerning Each Citizen woman or Man
And do all the mischief to others they Can

Then we want a few Boys Every night to go around
And throw Rocks at Houses and tear Fences Down
And make the night Hedious with yells & with Noise
For this is the use that we Have for the Boys.

And Especially Each Sunday Night they must make
All the Noise in their power to Keep people awake
Till the small Hours of night then to steal away Home
To see if their parents from meeting Have come.

Then we want a few women with the cunning and wise
To go through the settlements Telling their lies
And Stir up contention and Discord and strife
For in such a town it will give it New life

There is one thing Remaining to make it Complete
A grog shop some woman must start on the street.
To Deal out Bad whiskey Bad morals as well
Then the Town will be Ready to slide into Hell

Reality

At the schoolHouse below on Each Saturday night
The "People" all gather who wish to do Right
To Learn to be moral and Honest and wise.
And shun all bad Habits Contention and lies

It has been Read a few .5 of times of m' meeting and seemed
to give much satisfaction

They will Tell you to shun all your Chums on the street
No more on the Store steps or corners to meet
But study good Books and find pleasure at Home
And learn to be wise when you older have grown

They will Tell you to always be true to Each other
Be True to yourselves to your Father and mother,
They will Tell you to Honor your Parents and then
They'l be Proud of their Sons when they come to be men

They will tell you to shun all Contention and strife
So shun bad Companions & lead a New life
To be Kind to the poor and to all in Distress
It will make Home a Heaven it cannot do less

They will tell the young Ladies to Ever be true
To be Truthfull and Kind in whatever you do
Do in actions and words all the good that you Can
And you'll get for a Husband a good Honest man

There is one they Remaining to make it complete
A school House and Meeting House Built on the Street
They will Bring the fullfilement of Promises Given
And you will not go far to find you a Heaven

There are two paths before you in one you must go
One leads to Dishonor Perdition and woe
The other will lead you to Honor and Fame
And among Honest People an untarnished name

My Mother

Oh How my Heart yearns for a mothers Caresses
As when in my childhood by sickness laid low
When she Swept my wan face with her Dark Silken Tresses

And printed a kiss on my feverish Brow
Then tender and unwearing She watched by my Pillow
Till the long weary night with its Darkness had flown
And the Day God ascended oer mountain and Billow
And Relieved her night Vigils so patiently borne
How kind were Her accents How gentle her chiding
How sweet was Her smile and How fervent her prayers
Her love so unselfish So pure and abideing
How Patient her toiling How watchfull her care
The love of a mother abideth forever
It clings to the Heart when all others have flown
In all all of Earths Trials forget it No Never
No love like a mothers love Ever was known

Prayer

We thank thee oh God for the Springtime
That Spreads the green leaves on the trees
And scatters Bright Verdure around us
And fragrance on each swelling Breeze

We thank thee for Beautifull Summer
That Scatters the flowers on the plain
And Brings Gentle Zephyrs to fan us
And gives us Bright Sunshine and Rain

We thank thee for Frost laden Autumn
The Season of Harvest and Toil
When we lay up in store all the Riches
We have Garnered by the fruits of the soil

We thank thee for stern Hoary winters
The season that Nature must sleep
And lays up the snow in the mountains
That again - we a harvest may Keep

We thank thee that thou Hast provided
A place for thy Children to Hide
While the Scourges Pass over thee nations
Who will not they counsel, abide

We thank thee for Every Rich Blessing
So Bountiously Scattered around
Oh may we in meekness Receive them
And serving thee ears be Found

As Merry as a School Girl

As merry as a school girl I have often Heard them say
But I never knew its meaning untill this Very day
I saw her going Down the street with satchel on her arm
And Oh the merry song She sang it did my senses Charm

It Told me that her heart was light it told me she was free
From all the cares and ills of life that Haunted Such as me
It minded me of Bygone years when I was but a child
With Heart as free and pure as light and Spirits Just as wild

When I like Her was off to school with satchel on my arm
With not a care to grieve thy Heart but Everything to charm
But oh those Days are long since Past and life is nearly o'er
But oft I think of these Bright Days that will Return no more

Childhood

Oh Dont you Remember the Home of our childhood
That Bright sunny spot where we first saw the light
Where oft we have wandered over fields and over wild woods
No spot on the Earth Could to me be so Bright

Oh dont you Remember the the old Brown Cottage
The Kitchen the Square Room the Bed Room and all

The well at the Door and the orchard near bye it
The Garden the Barn and the corn House and all

Oh dont you Remember the old Dingy school House
With Benches and Desks all Defaced by the knife
Where we learned the first Lessons of Reading and Spelling
That has Marked out the way we have followed through life

Oh dont you Remember the old Kitchen fire place
Where oft we have met when our Days work was done
With Brothers and Sisters and friends we loved dearly
To pass off the Evening with all sorts of fun

Oh Dont you Remember our Dear loving mother
Who watched over our child hood so loving and true
Our fathers and mothers and sisters and Brothers
And every Bright token our infancy knew

Although im years have past and she has from it wandered
Yet often in fancys Bright Dreams I am there
Then Bright Rays of Happiness oer my fingers
As I gaze with Delight on the Vision so fair

Come Home

As I set by the fire I am Dreaming tonight
Of the years Past away that were Happy and Bright
When friends wife and children and all that was Dear
Around the old fireside were Clustering so near
Oh how Changed is the scene I am sitting alone
Except the two Children all others have gone
It is Late and Im lonely oh where are they be
Come Home Oh come Home to the children and me

Oh why will they leave the old cottage all day
The night is fast waning they still are away
The children are aweary and gone to their bed
I wish Mother would come many times they have said
I have Toiled all the day till I'm weary and sad
With no one to cheer me or make my Heart glad
But I'll watch over my children though lonely it be
Come Home oh come Home to thy children and me

Oh how vain are the Hopes and the Dreams of this life
How Dearly I've loved thee my children and wife
And Friends I have cherished Believing them True
They Have faded away Like the Bright morning Dew
Oh how fondly I've Hoped that this late would be mine
That friends would surround me in life sad Decline
That Peace and Contentment my fortune would be
Come Home oh Come Home to thy children and me

Fashion
There was a Time in Bygone years
   That I Remember well
When Fashion pride and Haughtiness
   In Utah Did not Dwell
When women spun and wove and made
   The Garments that they wore
And when they Knew what they had Cost
   They were Enjoyed the more

A neat Plain Dress of Homespun Then
   Was worn by one and all
And always was Deemed Good Enough
   For meeting or for Ball
The Hair god gave them then they wore
   With Neatness and with Grace

They never thought a Switch or Braid
    was needed in its place

Stays were not worn or Bustles then
    She was No Fashions Slave
But Every woman relied on
    The Form Her maker gave
The Home Her Husband Shared with Her
    Bedecked with Native Flowers
With Husband Children and with Friends
    She spent Her leisure Hours

Her Husbands love was all She asked
    To Him She freely gave
The Treasure of a womans love
    So fast Beyond the Grave
But Times have altered much since then
    The Noisy Spinning Wheel
That used to turn the wool to yarn
    Has Vanished with the Reel

The Loom that used to make the cloth
    Its Noise we Hear no more
And all the Clothes we Have to wear
    We Buy them at the store
Since fashion has been Introduced
    To make a womans Dress
She must Have twenty yards at least
    She cannot do with less

The Love She Bears Her Husband Now
    Is Measured by His Purse
And From its Contents to Her wants
    He is willing to Disburse
She has a smile for all she meets
    As She goes up or Down
Except His Husband and for Him
    She always wears a Frown

Yankee Doodle

Yankee Doodle is The Tune
    Sure Yankee chaps Invented
To sing on Independence Day
    And Make us Feel Contented
Now Independence Day Has come
    As Many Has before us
We'l sing Again The good old tune
    And You may join The Chorus
(Chorus) Yankee Doodle is The Tune
    The Mormons Find so Handy
    To sing on Independence Day
    Old Yankee Doodle Dandy

The Mormons are a Jolly Set
    They Come From Every Nation
From Every Country Every Clime
    In all This Broad Creation
They all Believe in Serving god
    Just as They are a Mind To

They all Believe that Washington
    The Founder of the Nation
Was called of God to Do that work
    And Did by Inspiration
They think the laws our fathers made
    Were what they were Intended
They've Stood the test a Hundred years
    And need not be amended
Chorus
There are some fellows now so smart
    They've got it in their noodles
The Mormon Boys can take no beat
    In Playing yankee Doodle
So they are trying Very Hard
    To Bust the Constitution
By Tearing up old Seventy Six
    And change the Constitution
Chorus
Then let us our own Business mind
    That is the Mormon Creed Sirs
And when the Race is Running Hard
    The Mormons in the lead Sirs
Then let them Marshal all their force
    We'll show the whole Caboodle
That we are Loyal Citizens
    To the Tune of yankee Doodle
'Tis the Last Apple Blossom
'tis the Last apple Blossom
    Left Blooming alone
All its Lovely Companions
    Are faded and gone

No Flower of its Kindred
    Remain to be found
They are faded away
    And Are Scattered arround
Ile not leave thee thou lone one
    To fade on thy tree
Where thy Beauty and fragrance
    All wasted would be
So fondly ile Pluck thee
    And Bear thee away
Where thy Beauty shall fade
    In a Fragrant Boquet

Our Boyhood Friends are Dying

Our Boyhood Friends are Dying
    For one by one they Go
The most of them are lying
    Beneath the sod so low
They are Resting from their labors
    The friends we loved so well
Along the Road we,or traveled
    Their mouldering Bodies Dwell

We sigh to see them leaving
    And sinking in the grave
Weve known them from our Boyhood
    Their Hearts were true and Brave
The good old friends we,or Cherished
    From Boyhoods Early Day
How can we Help but Shed a Tear
    To See them Pass away-

A few of them still wander
    Along Lifes Dreary way

But one by one they're leaving
  And Passing fast away
And soon Deaths Icy Hand
  Will Touch Each Heart so Brave
And Sink Each Friend of Boyhood
  Into a Silent Grave

And Thus Doth Time Draw wrinkly
  Where youths Bright Smile hath Played
The stars of Hope so once Twinkles
  Ere they begin to fade
We too are growing older
  Our locks are mixed with Grey
Ere many winters more
  We Too shall pass away

Then let us up and Doing
  And Battle in the Strife
To Finish up our Mission
  And do our Part in life
That when our work is Ended
  We'll know it is well Done
That we may Rest in Peace
  With all our Friends that's Gone

We have met we have parted like sisters and Brothers
And the Tie is made stronger that Binds to Each other
Thus may it be still when we meet and we Part
Till the Tie becomes strong that Endures around the Heart
Till we learn that we cannot be Happy alone
That we must have a peace in our Hearts for Each one
And the stronger the Tie the more Happy well be
Until we become as one great Family

My Brave Steed

Brave Steed thy work at last is Done
No more thy Nimble Feet
Will amble Oer the Pastures green
So graceful and so Fleet
Thou Hast Borne many a weary mile
Upon thy Sturdy Back
And always been my Hope and Stay
Upon the Desert Track

Thou Hast been Ever Brave and True
Thy Courage Did not Flee
And when my Life Endangered was
Thou Hast been True to me
When Dangers Lurked along my Path
Thy Fleetness Bore me Through
Well Could I trust my Noble Steed
For Thou wert Tried and True

Thou hast served me well for many years
Through many Dangers Passed
But age Come on and Cruel Death
Has Cut thee Down at last
No more Ile mount my Faithfull steed
To meet wild Dangers Dare

Jotting By The Way

My Mind Has been wandering Backward
Yes Back to the Land / my Birth
When tidings first Reached us that angels
Again had come back to the Earth
And Brought the glad news that Jehovah
His fullness day work had begun
And Brought Back the Priesthood to Joseph
This was in Eighteen thirty one

With Joy we Received the great tidings
That God. by His servents had Sent
And gave them a Home and a welcome
While they Preached to the People Present
And as we Believed in the Message
We Down to the waters Deed Go
to follow the steps of our Saviours
This was in eighteen thirty two

We Next came to Kirtland Ohio gather
The Saints there in numbers less four
That Joseph the prophet was with us
And his Hearts were as Soft and Stone
He taught us that if we were faithful
triumphant we always would be
our Enemies never would conquer
This was in Eighteen thirty three

The Elders were sent to the Nations
to spread the glad tidings abroad

And the Saints were Beginning to Gather
    To Build up the Kingdom of God
It was then we were Taught by the Prophet
    That God would Require of us sure
The Tithing to Build up His Kingdom
    This was in Eighteen Thirty Tens

He Taught us to love one another
    And never be Haughty or Vain
To leave off our Pride and Contention
    And from all bad Habits Refrain
We then to Gods name Built a Temple
    And all for His Blessings did Strive
And in it Received our Anointing
    This was in Eighteen Thirty Six

We then were Endowed with His Spirit
    The Gifts to the Saints were Restored
And many Received Revelation
    While the Tidings were Scattered abroad
The Saints were Increasing in Numbers
    But Joseph with others Did Fix
To Strengthen the Stakes in Missouri
    This was in Eighteen Thirty Six

Our Enemies Gathering around us
    Dissenters arose in our band
The Prophet with many more left us
    For Missouri our fair Promised land
With the Poor Saints we soon followed after
    By mobs from our Homes we were Driven
We traveled through Sickness and Sorrow
    This was in Eighteen Thirty Seven

And [illegible] and ourselves Left at Springfield
To care for the sick and the dead
While many Continued their journey
Although without money or Bread
But God gave us friends in our troubles
Who Watched with us Early and Late
Until we Had from sickness Recovered
This was in Eighteen Thirty Eight

The saints from Missourie were Driven
From all their possessions to Roam
And the Scudders Had crossed over the River
At Commerce to find a new Home
Then again we were traveling, Westwards
To finish our formar Design
To Dwell with the Saints and the Prophet
This was in Eighteen Thirty Nine

At Commerce the Saints Did gather
To Build up the City Nauvoo
On the Banks of the Great Mississippi
A Beautifull City Soon Grew
For the Saints that were Scattered Did Rally
To Build them new Homes Soon Began
So awhile they Grew Rich and Did prosper
This was in Eighteen Forty One

We then Built a Town called it Ramus
A Branch some twenty miles from Nauvoo
Where they we met with the Prophet
Who Taught us Some things that we knew
It was there that by I learned the great Secret
Which then was Revealed to but few

Many wives we should Marry if faithfull
    This was in Eighteen forty Six
D[illegible]

Dissenters Soon Sprang up amongst us
    Like Judas our Prophet Betrayed
Among them were those He had Trusted
    And Placed in High Places to Lead
They Scattered the Seeds of Dissention
    But Soon from our Midst they Did Flee
To Stir up the Ire of the Gentiles
    This was in Eighteen forty Three.

We again Built a Temple at Nauvoo
    By Toil it was finished at Last
But Traitors and Mobs gathered Round us
    And the Prophet in Prison was cast
Then Joseph and Hyrum were Murdered
    Their Blood Stains the Carthage Jail floor
So Come up in Judgment against them
    This was in Eighteen forty four.

Then our Enemies poured in the City
    To pillage and Plunder and Rob
And Many Crossed over the River
    And Left Everything to the Mob
Then Brigham was Chosen our Leader
    As they now were Determined to Drive
With a few He Crossed over the River
    This was in Eighteen forty five

At Kanesville and old Winter Quarters
They Stopped and for winter, did set
To the Spring to continue their Journey
This was in Eighteen Forty Six

The Saints still Remaining at Nauvoo
Were Leaving us fast as they Could
To follow their friends to the Mountains
When they could Get Clothing and food
They scattered abroad through the country
In winter by Mobs they were Driven
To find a new home in the mountains
This was in Eighteen Forty Seven

Then Traitors Set fire to the Temple
Which Quickly Burned Down to the Ground
To Serve as a witness against them
On the Day when the Trumpet shall Sound
But the few that Remained in the City
As the Season was Getting so late
Concluded to Winter at Nauvoo
It was in Eighteen Forty Eight

Then I think of the Sad Desolation
We met with in passing around
The Beautiful City in Ruins
The Temple Burned Down to the Ground
The Prophet and Patriarch Murdered
Destruction before and behind
The saints Driven out in the Desert
It was thus in Eighteen Forty Nine

In the Spring we moved Forward to Kanesville
But found them in Sorrow and Gloom

The cholera swept through the Country
And many went Down to the Grave
But we toiled on through Sickness and Sorrow
Till the Time for Departure had come
To Follow the Saints to the Mountains
This was in Eighteen Fifty one

When our long weary Journey was over
Our Trials of Travel were past
We had Reached our Dear Homes in the Mountains
To Dwell with our Brethren at last
Since Twenty nine years we have Toiled
In Building up Zions Strong holds
In the year Eighteen Hundred and Eighty
The Church is just Fifty years old

And where are those Brave Valiant Heroes
Who have Followed their Leaders so Long
And Fought the good Fight for the Kingdom
When the Battle was Raging so Strong
A few are Remaining Amongst us
The Most of them Sleep By the way
They were Brave Martyrs of Jesus
To come forth in the great Coming Day

It soon will be my Turn to Follow
And lie down a season to Rest
To arise with the Saints and the Prophet
In that Far Brighter land of the Blest
Then Ill claim the Bright Promise He gave me
With Hands on my Head long ago
A Kingdom And crown when Id Finished
The work I on Earth had to do

144

It is thirty three years since we started
   Our wilderness Journey to make
So arrive at the End of our Journey
   Just Seven years more it will Take
And those who hold out and are faithfull
   No more from their Homes will be driven
But Build and Inherit the Kingdom
   In the year Eighteen Eighty Seven.

The Pick Nick

We are a Band of little Children
   From Sunday School we come
So Join You in your Pick Nick
   And Have a little Fun
We'l Speak and Sing before you
   And do the best we can
So make the Day Pass Merrily
   According to your Plan

But we Hope you will Remember
   We all are Very young
And when we all Have Spoken
   Recited and Have Sung
You will Please Excuse our Blunders
   For we is trying Hard to learn
And Hope on this occasion
   Your Kind applause to Earn

Our Parents are before us
   Our Friends and Teachers Dear
Tis Hard for us to Speak or Sing
   And Stand before you there
But Since you wish and try to do
   The best that we know How

Arizona

The Home I long Have Cherished is Home no more for me
I am weary of its Toiling its want and misery
   For there, a better Land I Know
   Where Trees Bears Fruit and crops will Grow
Away in arizona Oh thats the Land for me

For many years I've Labored While youth and strength was (mine
To try to Lay up something to use in Life Decline
   But all is gone and I a poor
   To Drive the grim wolf from my Door
Ile go to arizona Oh thats the Land for me

The years are Growing on me and Times are Harder still
I meet with many a Jostle in going down the Hill
   But yet Ile try while Life Remain
   To make a Happy Home again
Away in Arizona Oh thats the Land for me

Then come Dear Friends and Kindred and let us Leave This Land
And find a better country to colonize our Band
   With better Climate Better Soil
   Where we can Reap the Fruits of Toil
Away in arizona Oh thats the Land for me

The Old Home

I have tilled many years on this Small Spot of ground
In the Hopes to Raise something to Last the year Round
To Lay Bye for winter my children to feed
But have never as yet Raised the worth of my seed

I have Plowed I have Harrowed the Plowed and Sowed
And many a Day I have watered and Hoed
I have Toiled all the Summer and when in the fall
I have Looked for my Crop There was Nothing at all

For the Land is so poor and the water so low
That the Land would get Hard and the crop would not grow
So I get for my Toil very little or none
And I always must Buy what I ought to have grown

Then there is my Orchard the largest in Town
I have often been Tempted to cut the trees Down
They Blossom to make me believe they will Bear
When I look for the fruit in the fall There's none there

In the Spring all the fruit by the frost will be Killed
And the Land is so poor Tis not fit to be Tilled
So I Toil all the summer for Nothing at all
And must buy what I count to Say Bye in the fall

Time is Precious

Time is Precious use it wisely
   Idle not the Hours away
Years are made of little moments
   Grasp and use them while you may
Time is Fleeting Every moment
   Let some Noble work be Done
When Tis past Tis gone forever
   Years are flying one by one

Every moment there is Something
   That your Hands may find to do
Short will brighten Some ones Burden
   And a Blessing Bring to you

There are always those arround you
    That may need your Help or care.
Sinking Hearts are always near you
    For the Poor are Everywhere

Feed the Hungry Clothe the Needy
    Kindness to the poor Import
Gentle words that cost you Nothing
    Often Raise the sinking Heart
Never Falter in well Doing
    Labor with your Hands and Brain
Kind words Spoken to The Erring
    Sometimes Bring them back again

When the years of Life are numbered.
    And your sun is Nearly Set
Leave no Stains in Life behind you
    That may cause you Sad Regret
Let your Life be Spent in doing
    Good to all and Harm to none
That you Calmly may Resign it
    Knowing all Has been well Done

Mothers Birth Day

Dear mother we are Happy to meet Here again
Neath the old Cottage Roof where So oft we have been
In Pleasure and Joy may the time Pass away
And may it be to you a Happy Birth Day

We have thrown away care a few moments to come
Our Kindred to meet in the old Cottage Home
Then Let us Have Joy while together we Stay
May Happiness Reign on our mothers Birth Day

Though Time Has made wrinkles that makes me less fair
And Snow flakes are scattered all over my Hair
Though my sight may be dim and my hands growing cold
Yet the Heart is still young though the Body is old

Then away with dull care let us live while we live
And Enjoy Every pleasure life to us can give
Let us smile when we should thus our Sorrow war Pain
But often find time to be children again

What is Home without the Children
What is Home without the children
Prattling Round the Cottage Hearth
With their Eyes serene Beaming
Full of Laughter Joy and mirth

Tiny Fingers Bent on mischief
    Never Still from morn Till night

Without Children Home is lonely
    How we miss their Noisy mirth
How we miss their Gentle footsteps
    Crowding Round our lonely Hearth
How we miss their noisy prattle
    How we miss their childish glee
How we miss their fond Caresses
    As they Sit upon our Knee

When the Evening Shadows gather
    And our Daily Toil is over
How we miss their Noisy Greeting
    At our Humble Cottage Door
Heaven Bless the Darling Children
    Though they need our Constant care
They will be the Brightest Jewels
    In the Crown we Hope To wear

God Bless The Children

The little ones are coming I Hear their Noisy feet
I Hear their Noisy Prattle as they come down the Street
They are coming Down to Grand Pas our Hens or us to Stay
To tumble in the orchard & around the old Hours play

They will pull the things to pieces and scatter them about
They will make the old Time music the children Laugh and Sh
They will be in Every mischief their little Hands can find
They Know I'd scold a little Bit that they do not mind

Their father and their mother How short the Time to me
Since they were little children and sitting on my Knee

God Bless the little Children long may they live to come
To cheer the lonely Cottage that was their Parents Home
While it Remain their Presence will ever welcome be
And when I'm gone they'l miss me and shed a tear for me

Sweet Rose

Sweet Rose in thy Fragrance and Beauty I found thee
When all thy dear kindred had faded away.
When cold dreary winter was howling around thee
And Frost on thy petals like Diamonds did Play.

Sweet flower i'le not leave thee to Pine in thy Beauty
To wither and Die by the Frost in a Day.
i'le take thee where kind gentle Beauty caress thee
And Nurse thee to life till thy fevers dies away.

The Hoodlums

The Hoodlums are abroad tonight
  I Hear them on the Square
I know them By their Vulgar Talk
  I Hear them Curse and Swear
I Hear their whistle and their yell
  That tells the place to meet
And woe unto the Reckless lass
  who is late upon the Street
And woe unto the Sonsie Vicar
  They'l lay them low tonight
And woe unto the window panes
  Whereer they See a light
Destruction follows in their path

To any Female who may Dare
Their Haunts to Venture Near

The Little ones

The little ones are back again
  I hear their Noisy feet
They make the old House Ring again
  With Childrens Music Sweet
I love to Hear their Boisterous Shout
  I love their Noisy yell
I love to Hear their merry laugh
  Tis Music sweet to me
I know they Ramble through the House
  I know they Mischief find
I know they tear things upside Down
  But that I do not mind
For Then Ile scold the little ones
  Which makes them love me more
And makes me Dream of Happy Days
  That will Return no more
Of Days when this old Cot was new
  And around this Lonely Hearth
Were Children who could Mischief do
  And Shout with Noisy Mirth
They've gone & left this Home and me
  In sorrow to Remain
But oft they Send their little ones
  To make me Dream again

Our Sunday School

We are little children Happy are we
Every Sabbath morning Here we will be
  Learning ours Lessons well
  Learning the truth to tell

Learning to Read and Spell A B C
Bright Happy faces meet with us Here-
In our Pleasant School Room we love so Dear
Learning our Hearts to do
All that is Good and true
With the Great End in View which is so ?
Here we meet our School mates filled with Delight
Here we meet our Teachers Smiling so Bright
Hearts filled with joy to day
Listening to what they say
Teaching the Narrow way Teaching the Right-

To Neddy

On your Mission Dear Brother be Faithfull and true
The saints Here in Zion are Praying for you
That God will Protect you by His mighty Hand
While you se Spreading the truth in your own Native land

We know that temptation will lie in your way
We know of the trials you meet with Each day
But if you are Faithfull and firmly will Stand
You will bring many souls from your own native land

We know of the Poverty Samuel and woe
In the land where your duty has called you to go
But Friends will Surround you and God By you stand
And Bless you with Health in your own Native land

And when the time comes you will get your releace
You will come back to Zion with Honor and Peace
Take your wife and your children and friends by the Hand
And bring many souls From your own Native land.

Laura's Birth Day

To day is your Twenty First Birth Day they say
And Happy I Hope you Have been .
And as each year Goes Round may you Happiness e
Till your years Number three Score and ten .
Billies Storms you've known in the years that are Past
May your future be Happy and Bright
And as years Come and go may the sun light your Path
May your Heart in the future be light —

Sabbath Morning

It is pleasant on each Sabbath morning to meet
In our Dear sunday school our Companions to Greet
And Hear the Kind words of our Teachers So Dear
Who are trying to learn us Gods name to Revere

We are Happy to meet you and Hope that we may
Learn How to be wiser and better Each Day
And may we in Honor and Virtue and truth
Continue To grow while we are still in our youth

It is Pleasant to Listen while teachers Explain
The great truths of Heaven on Earth one again
That we may be usefull as older we Grow
To work in the Kingdom of god Here below

When we have grown older and Battling for truth
We shall Ever Remember the Scenes of our youth
Our Dear Sunday School and our Teachers so Kind
Their names in our Thought we shall ever to mind

Dance on the Brain

Oh what a condition the people are in

They Rave about Dancing the Symtims are plain
They all are affected with Dance in the Brain

They gather bye the es on corner and street
And talk aloud Dancing with Each one they meet
But they never agree So they argue in vain
For they all are affected with Dance on The Brain

The women have got it so bad they will go
To a Dance all alone through the mud and the snow
No matter How Hard it may Snow sleet or Rain
They will go for they all Have got Dance on the Brain

And when They get there they the music will Curse
And say its so bad That I cannot be worse
They will swear they will never Dance by it again
But its all in they Eye theyve got Dance on the Brain

they will say that their money for nothing theyve p—
And they Never again Such a fool will be made
But the Very next Dance they are Ready again
To wade through the mud theyve Got Dance on the B—

They will call the Comittee and Bishops unfair
For saying they shall not Drink whiskey and swear
And from a few o this bad Habits Refrain
When they know Very well theyve got Dance on the B—

Never Give up

There are Times in our Lives when in Darkness and glo—
Our minds are overshadowed as Dark as the Tomb
When joy Hope and gladness have faded away
And left us in Sadness to grief and dismay

But do not Despair or at fortune be whining
For Every Dark Cloud Has a Bright Silver Lining

Altho = Fortune is fickle and Friends are untrue
And the fates are against you and Pleasures are few
Altho Dark are the clouds that hang over thy way
Press on Do not Heed what the Tempter may Say
    Dont falter or Stumble or Ever be Pining
    For the Darker The Cloud is the Brighter the Lining

Though your friends may be few and your problems a close
Look arround you will see those where fate is severe
Tis to Teach us this Lesson that trials we meet
If we Taste not the Bitter we Know not the Sweet
    Be Patient the Sun will soon Brightly be Shining
    And show you The Cloud Had a Bright silver lining

To Nellie

Dear girl you have wished me a Happy New year
When the Day was far Spent and the End was so near
Tis an Emblem of Life and Reminds me so plain
But a few more short years I Shall with you Remain

We'll follow our Leader the Brave old Tradition
And for his Aid De Camps we will have Superstition
These Priest craft and Predjudice Falsehood and lies
Will join to assist us in the great Enterprise.

Then Bigotry Slander and Gossip and Tattle
Assurance and Impudence join in the Battle
With all these great allies he surely will win
And crush out these mormons and make them give in

We know all the world these great leaders will Follow
And all they may say they will greedily Swallow
Then come on ye Heroes and join in the Cry
We'll put Down these Mormons we'll conquer or Die

We know that old Truth will Command their Loyalty
And Reason and Justice will come to their aid
But force and Oppression will Arrive in my Van
And they will assist us and Do all they Can

Their weapon the Bible they take at its word
Is keener by far than a two edged Sword
We know they can wield it and in a fair fight
They Quickly will put Every traitor to flight

But there we shall mainly depend upon might
While they will Depend upon one they call Right
Upon these two Heroes the fight will Depend
And if they should aim it our glory will End

Our Leader Tradition we bye him have stood
And Fought North H's Banner through Rivers of Blood
Once more we cry Just Hope Now if we should fail
Ah yes they Have Conquered and truth will Prevail

Rejoice oh ye Nations Tradition is Dead
And all the Brave allies so long it has lead
In prison must he Never more to come forth
While Truth will Prevail and Spread over the Earth

My 58th Birth Day

How fleet the years are Passing Bye
That Brings us Nearer to the Close
When in the grave we all must lie
Where we shall find our last Repose

Another year has passed and gone
And I am fifty Eight years old
Adown the stream I do Totter on
A few more years and all is told

God grant that Peace may be my lot
The time that still to me is given
That I may do His will on Earth
And meet the friends I love in Heaven

The Old Brown Cot

I love it I love it and who would not
Tis the place I was born in that old Brown cot
It was there that I set on my mothers Knee
When she Rocked me to sleep with Her Bye Baby

It was there that she learned me Her Dear name to speak
As she steadied my foot steps so tottering and weak
Where she taught me the lessons of Honor and truth
And Virtue and love in the Days of my youth

For many long years I have wandered away
From that Dear Cherished spot Till my Hair has grown grey

But I'll Never forget it where ever I be
The Place where I set on my Dear mothers Knee

To Naoma

She has lain down to sleep she at last is at Rest
And Her spirit has gone to the land of the Blest
Where Her Husband is waiting to welcome Her Home
To meet with her Friends who before Her have gone.

We miss Her but why should we wish her to stay
To linger where Sorrow Encircles her way
She has Fought the good Fight and the Victory won
She has finished Lifes work and we know tis well done

She Has gone from our Presence but why should we weep
When we Know that we Too soon must lie Down to Sleep
Then we'd meet Her again in that Bright Sunny Home
With our Kindred and friends who before us have gone

The Loafer

Who Saunters out upon the Street
To laugh and chat with those He meets
And light and smoke His Segarette
                        The Loafer

And when he finds a Pleasant Shade
That some good Neighbors trees have made
Who sits and plies His Pocket Blade
                        The Loafer

Who sits and smokes and whittles on
Until his Segarette is gone
And then he makes another one
                        The Loafer

To some ones House it's own 'tis not
                    The Loafer,

When seated in an Easy Chair
He makes so free you would Declare
That He must be the governer, there
                    The Loafer

In Flattery He will Excell
And many silly Stories Tell
And Laugh and Gossip too as well
                    The Loafer

His patient wife at Home must stay,
To Toil and Labor all the Day
While He is Idling Time away
                    The Loafer

She Tries to keep Her children Neat
And Furnish them with Food to Eat
While He is Lounging up the Street
                    The Loafer,

Our Pleasure Ride

We took a Ride the other day
To Salt Creek Canon Bent our way
        To Have a Little Pleasure.
For we Had Heard of mellons there
And we Had Cash and Time to Spare
        And thus we Spent our Leisure
At one o,clock the Team appeared.
The Driver Shouted all aboard
        And Quickly we were Jogging
The Horses traveled Like the wind
And Quickly Left the Town behind
        Without a bit of Flogging
We Jolted up and Jolted Down
And Every Rock or Ditch we Found
        But then we Did not mind them

For we Had Mellons on the Brain
As Big as Pumpkins that was plain
        When we got there to find them
At Half past two we Reached the place
And Quickly Right about Did fall
        And went to see about them
But Disappointment we must meet
The Mellons were not large or sweet
        So we must do without them
Except a few we took to show
We did to Salt Creek Canon Go
        If any, one should Doubt it
At Nine o'clock we all got Home
The children all rejoicing Came
        And this is all about it

Cold Winter

Cold winter is coming There's Frost in the air
    The Beautyfull Summer is Past
The Flowers are all Dying that once was So fair
    Their fragrance Has gone with the Blast
The Tops of the mountains are covered with Snow
    The North wind is Passing your door
Then if you Have plenty to Pay as you go —
    Be Sure to Remember the Poor

Cold winter is coming Its footsteps are near
    To spread Desolation around
And make the Earth Dreary and Furly and sere
    And Scatter the snow on the ground
The Leaves are Beginning to fall from the trees
    The Beautifull Harvest is over
The Beautifull Streams are Beginning to Freeze
    Tis the time to Remember the Poor

Cold winter is coming where plenty abounds
  The Dance and the Song will be Heard
With merth and with Music your Halls will Resound
  And Luxury Shine on your Board
Then Remember the Poor let their Hearts be made glad
  With something you give from your Store
It will Comfort the Feeble and Cheer up the sad
  The Little you give to the poor

Cold winter is coming it's Cold Frosty Breath
  Is whistling oer Mountain and Dell
All nature Hid South with the finger of Death
  And lock up the Earth with his Spell
He will laugh at the needy that knock at the poor
  As widely He opens their Door
Then let us be Mindful to keep Him away
  With Charity Comfort the poor

The Old Fogy

They can call me old Fogy whenever they will
Or stereotyped merman for good or for ill
Such names to another might give an offence
But to me it shows lacking of good Common Sense

I am proud to inform them for many long years
I have waded through sorrow affliction and fears
And I've stood by the side of the prophet of god
When mobs and when traitors were seeking his blood

And many a time I have sat Neath his Voice
When the words He has spoken has made me rejoice
When He taught us the lessons of Right and of Truth
I have treasured them up since the Days of my youth

When He told of the times" "were near to our Door
Of the Blessings that god for the saints Had in store
Of Sorrows of Happiness Joys and of tears
Not one sentence Has failed I have watched many years

But He,s left us and gone to the mansions above
To Prepare us a Home if we faithful should Prove
But the words He Has Spoken while life shall Remain
Will be lamps to my feet till I meet Him again

And I ever will Cherish His memory Dear
Till I finish The Mission He left for me Here
Then call me old Fogy I'll make no Complaint
When it means an old latterr latter day saint

Zion

Oh ye pleasant Vales and ye Mountain Dales
    Of this Dear Chosen Land
Oh ye Chrystale Rills and ye Snow cupped Hills
    That murmer over the Sand
Oh ye Happy Homes where Saints Have come
    To do His Holy will
To Learn His ways And Sing His praise
    And all His Laws fullfill
Oh ye waving Grain where the Desert Plain
    Now Blossoms like the Rose
Where a chosen Band From Every Land
    Now Dwell in Sweet Repose
Oh ye Happy Land where Temples Stand
    From which His Laws Go forth
While Sin and Crime in Every Clime
    Is Swept from off the Earth
Here Christ again will come and Reign
    A thousand years below

And Peace and Joy without alloy
  To Every Heart will flow
Then ye pleasant vale & ye mountain side   And some in one...
O come in joy such...   ...and eternity

Our Mothers Birth Day

Tis your Birthday again How the time flies away
  How swiftly the years come and go
How short seems the time since that Bright Happy day
  When we met Here just one year ago

But the Day Has arrived not so fair as before
  For the Children Have wandered away
And the few that Remain Have but little to spare
  To make cheerful and Brighten the day
But our thoughts linger with you and we Hope it may be
  Our lot when another shall Come
So all be Joyathers and pass off the Day
  With Joy in the old Cottage Home
Then may there be many Bright Birth Days to come
  With Children and Friends ever n or
To cheer up and Brighten the old Cottage Home
  Your Spirits to comfort and cheer

The Mail Corsier

Oh yes the Days are growing short
  At Six the Sun goes Down
I take my Sack and Haste away
  To meet the Southern Bound
When at the Track I sit me Down
  Upon the Iron Rail
And wait alone the train to come
  To Bring me up the Mail
Adown the track along the gloom
  With anxious look I gaze
Until I see the smoke arise
  Above the Twilight Haze

Two minutes more the train arrives
    The Mailman without fail
Receives my sack and then in turn
    He Passes out my mail
With Sack across my Shoulder then
    I for the office start
No matter if the Roads are bad
    No matter if tis Dark
For well I Know theyre waiting there
    They Never Never fail
So expecting Round the office Door
    Until I Bring the mail
And if a letter fail to come
    The mail man Bears the Blame
And he must listen to their Slurs
    As if He'd stolen the same
And when the Papers Day arrives
    Of corse it should not fail
But if it Does some fault of His
    Has Kept it from the mail
He must be Ready Night and day
    To wait on one and all
He must not leave the place one Hour
    For fear some one might call
But He must be a Public Slave
    To Please all or its Fail
For the Honor of the office Buys
    For attending to the mail

The Mail of this Town

The mail of this Town is a wonderfull mail
That is Brot to the office Each night from the Rail
For the people will Gather from all parts of Town
To Hear what the News is and Swallow it Down

When the Sack is unlocked and the mail is Turned out
The people Stand waiting both Indoors and out
For the calling of Names which is Done without fail
For they Each one Expect to get something by mail

Theres a Bundle of letters Tied up with a String
And a few Scandent papers No very great thing
But they watch the proceeding as if Swould Entail
A Fortune to Just git one letter by mail

Then Theres The Enquirer The News Deseret
The Herrald and tribune I must Not forget
They Bring us the News whether Current or stale
Twice a week we are sure to find them in the mail

The names are soon Called and the mail Handed out
Just about one in Ten get a letter No Doubt
Now the Rest will go Home to be back without fail
Tomorrow to See who gets letters by mail

Cottage Home

I ow a Humble Cottage Home
    Where the Summer Flowers Bloom (seven
And an orchard with an azure Neath its Bow old
I ow a garden for the Hoe
    Where I watch plow and sow
And a little farm above for the plow Old Friend

I've a Parlor and a Hall
    If a Friend Should Chance to Call
And a wish within the Cottage to Reside Old Friend
    I Have Children living Near
    The Old Cottage Home to Cheer
And dve friends who Dwell around on Every side Old Frnn
    I am sit within my Door
    When my Daily Toil is oer
And be thankfull for the Blessings in my Reach Old Frnn
    And I think Though light of Purse
    That my Fate might still be worse
And I Proffit by the lessons it Does Teach Old Friend
    I have cast away my Pride
    And Base Flattery beside
And I try to gather wisdom from above Old Friend
    Then if you like my Style
    Just call in and sit awhile
And I'll tell you what I Hate and what I love old Frnn
    I love a womans voice
    When She makes Kind words Her choice
And the Prattle of The Children at their play old Friend
    But I Hate a scold and shrew
    Who find nothing Else to do
But to tattle and make mischief all the Day Old Friend
    I love an Honest man
    Who is doing all He can
So Promote the joy and Happiness of Earth old Friend
    But I Hate the Selfish Cuss
    Who would Rob you of your Purse
And will Leave the Earth no better for His birth old Friend
    I love a well tried Friend
    Upon whom I can Depend
Who will kindly Bring my Faults to my View Old Friend

But a flatterer I Dispise
  Who with flattery and lies
Serves all with whom He has to do Old Sound

To Mary Ann

Dear Sister I'm thinking of years past away
  And of Scenes in the Land of our Birth
When we little children together Did Play
  And we knew not the sorrows of Earth

Your Parents so kind I Remember them well
  Their love you had no one to Share
Death took them and left you many strangers to Dwell
  An Orphan with no Kindred near

But you found in my Mother a friend Kind and true
  You loved Her as well as your own
She cared for your wants like a Mother to you
  Until you a woman Had Grown

Your life has been Chequered with joy and with care
  But friends you have always found near
And the years that are Past have Dropped She on you (Hem
  to show you the End Draweth near

May the years Still Remaining be Happy and Bright
  And may there be many to come
When you are finished this work and have found the End (Bright
  May you know it has all been well Done.

I am Waiting Here For Thee

The years of life are waning fast
  Their Fall will soon be o'er

I soon shall Reach the other Shore
for I am growing old
I seem to Hear my mothers Voice
a whispers unto me
Be faithful till thy work is Done
I'm waiting Here for thee

My feeble limbs my furrowed Brow
My Hair fast turning grey
My sight grows Dim my Hearing Dull
All tokens of Decay
And whisper with their gentle Voices
Which Plainly says to me
Your friends upon the other Side
Are waiting there for thee

My friends of youth are nearly gone
They have fallen By the way
I seldom see a face I knew
In youths Bright sunny Day
Theyve left me but I seem to Hear
Them whisper back to me
Toil on and finish up thy work
Were waiting Here for thee
A. Duett

Bup You girls may Dress up in great splendor
And Innocent look as a lamb
So try to Entrap Some poor fellow
But we know it is nothing but sham
You may Put on your Diamonds and lace
Your gew gaws and Riblons so gay
You may Paint up and double your faces
But youl never catch me in that way

Girls Well now I declare Did you Ever
  You Realy get worse Every Day
You think You can do as you Please sirs
  And we women have nothing to say.
We Realy would Like you to know sirs
  We will not be Bossed about thus
We women will do as we Please
  And will Dress if it Does make a fuss

Boys You lie in your bed in the morning
  Till ten for you must have some sleep
For you did not get Home from the party
  Till Day was beginning to Peep
You go moping about in the parlor
  From all usefull labor you shirk
And you spend Half your time doing Nothing
  While your mother is Doing the work

Girls Now Realy are you any better
  You Drink chew and Smoke and you swear
And you spend Half your time on the Corners
  At Each woman that passes to Stare.
You make love to Each one that will let you
  And Mercy what Lies you can tell
And in the Fine Clothes you are not paid For
  You think you are cutting a Swell

Then let us be Happy together
And leave off contention and Strife
For who could enjoy this life Snug
Clasp't as a Husband & Wife

To, Joseph

I Know it would be Idle words
To Bid you not to weep
As Her you've laid Beneath the sod
To take Her final sleep.
As we are Doomed to Bear the Pang
Of sorrow Here below
And when with Dearest friends we part
The Bitter, tears will flow
But there's a Hope is still sincere
That whispers to your Heart
And tells you of a better Home
For those with whom we part
As tells you that few years at best
Can to this Life be given
Then we shall meet with those we love
And Dwell with them in Heaven
Then let this thought Inspire your Heart
To Banish Doubts and fear
And give you Strength to Bear the pang
And Help you Dry your tears
And in the years that still Remain
To give you joy and peace
And Help you in your deeply toil
And Happiness increase

The Home of my Boyhood

The Home of my Boyhood the place of my Birth
It is Dearer to me than all others on Earth
Its Charm is still with me wherever I Roam
I can never forget thee my own Boyhood Home

The Dear loving mother who watched oer my youth
And taught me the Lessons of Honer and Truth
Her voice in my fancy in accents so low
Is whispering to me whereever I go

The voice of my father still sounds in my ears
The Laugh of my Brothers and Sisters so Dear
The Cow Bells low jingle the old Dinner Horn
The Crow of the Cock to awake us Each Morn

The Hoot of the owl and the lone whippoorwill
At Evening we Heard from the woodland and Hill
They still Ring in my ears altho long years have pass
Since I saw the Dear Home of my Infancy past

Although many a mile I have wandered away
My Body Grows feble my Hair turning Grey
The Happy scenes linger I Dream of them yet
The Home of my Boyhood I'll never forget

Seard For Mother

Oh John there is something the matter I'm sure
    With Poor little Baby today
It has slept all the morning so sweet and demure
    When you know it should wake up and Play
I went to the cradle to listen just now
    And see if the clothes did not smuther

At the old cottage Home By the fireside alone
    Sits mother Dejected and sad
She is thinking of years that forever are gone
    When the little ones made Her Heart glad
The Door opens softly a Voice in her Ear
    Says Baby Has something the Bothers
They could not Decide what the matter could be
    So They told me to Hurry for mother

There,s a light in Her Eye as she wakes from the cold
    She mutters, Perhaps it is Best
But they settled till they lift till it so weary and Old
    I should think they might now let me Rest
But the yearn has Disposed there,s a bright new trust
    No matter, How stormy the weather
When the children Have settled She,s Ready to Start
    And she,s Glad when they Send for their mother

For she knows that Her Presence will Banish their gloom
    And Drive away sorrow and fear,
And scatter the sunlight and cheer up the Home.
    They are safe when their mother is near
Ah sad is the Home where no mother may Come
    Its Unselfish troubles to smother
And lighten the Burdens and Trials of Home
    God Bless every Dear loving mother

To David

I have made up my mind you had best trend your ways
And come and Spend with yours old friends a few days

Put in a few Blankets a little clean Hay
And come and spend with us our Fathers Birth Day

Bring with you the children those who can leave Home
And Mary ann too if she wishes to come
And other good Friends you may meet on the way
And Have a good time on our Mothers wedding Day

Bring with you some game say a goose or a Duck
And a lot of good fish if yours Having good luck
And anything Else that may come in the way
To make a good time on our sisters Birth Day

A gun to kill game with for some of the Boys
Or the geese that fly over and make such a noise
Say Fathers old Bet If you think it would Pay
For No Doubt you Remember He died on that Day

Perhaps if you Happen to come by Spring Lake
Some others may join you a visit to make
If so they'l be welcome as long as they stay
To make a good time on our girls wedding Day

What shall our Christmas Dinner be
yankee A Pumpkin Pie a Turkey Roast
A Pudding of Corn meal
A Mug of cider Ginger Bread Pork chickens pie and veal
This Bill of Fare will do for me
This shall our Christmas Dinner be
Englishman
Roast Beef Plum pudding and stale Bread
A Veal or mutton Pie
A mutton chop a mug of ale and whiskey from the Rye
This Bill of Fare &c

12th Day of June My Fathers Birth Day and Wedding Day my Sisters Birth Day my Daughters Wedding Day Old Bet a Keepsake My fathers old Flint Lock Shot gun

Frenchman
A mutton pie a roast steel A pidgeon Duck or snipe
Good Pastry Tarts a little wine with Chicken fish & Tripe
Chorus   This Bill of fare &c

Dutchman Sourkrout and Cabbage Mutton Pie a pot of Beer or ale
Fat Beef and cheese and Buttermilk and Bread a little to eat
Chorus

Irishman Potatoes Buttermilk and Pork a Sort of Oat meal Bread
Good whiskey Gin and ale & Beer Cheese Beef & Herring Red
Chorus

Scotchman Fat beef and pork & mutton pie Potatoes Cabbage Veal
A glass of whiskey Beer or ale and Bread of good oat meal
Chorus

Welchman Roast Beef Plum pudding chicken Pie Potatoes Bread & Ham
Tea coffee ale a little wine Fresh Pork and Veal or Lamb
Chorus

Norwegian Good fat Reindeer and Fish and Seal
Will make for me a Splendid meal
Chorus

Indian Parch corn Dried Venison Game and fish
It's Just as good as I can wish
Chorus

Negro Fat Opossum Coon and Hominy
And Hoe Kake & good Enough for me
Chorus

Canabal A Missionary is good Enough
We Boil them when they're Old and Tough

To my Brother B J J

Dear Brother in thinking of years past away
When we were at Home with our mother
Who loved us so faithfully kindly and true
And taught us to love one another

She Taught us good Precepts she gave good advice
    She proved our best Friend to the last.
But How have we Heeded the lessons she taught
    As on through this life we have passed
We sometimes have Differed and Passions would Rise.
    We have Quarrelled and strove with Each other
And often the sun has gone Down on wrath.
    We learned not these lessons from Mother
Now as age has come on we are Nearing the End.
    If our lives we take time to look over
Perhaps we may see a few places to mend
    Ere we meet Her on yonders Bright shore
Then let us Blot out from our lives all the past
    And by all the Future to Brighten
Perhaps it may prove a good lesson at last
    And Help us our Burdens to brighten.

To My Sister Almera
Dear Sister long years Have Passed By since we met
But thy form and thy Features I do not forget
And perhaps in the picture I send you may see
Some Token or sign to Remind you of me
The glass No Doubt tells you that age comes to you
The Picture will show you I am growing old Too.
And we know that Ere many more years shall Pass By
That we both in the grave for a season must lie
Then Ere the time comes we must lie down to Rest.
In the cold silent grave Let us Bury the past
In the years that Remain let us Bear with Each other
And live By the precepts laid Down by our mother
And if on the Earth we shall not meet again
May we meet in that land where no sorrow or pain
Shall mar our Enjoyment when life shall be over
May we meet with our friends who have gone on before

To my Brother William

Dear Brother the picture you sent me
  I am sure it no better could be
It is Really so very much like you
  It seems to be speaking to me
Tis a present I long have been wanting
  A place in my album to fill
I have shown it to all of the children
  All say it is Dear Uncle Will

Keep of my thanks for the present
  It is all I have now to Bestow
And if you could know how we prize it
  You would not be sorry I know
The woman who stands up Besides you
  Her Features and form is so plain
The children as soon as they saw it
  Says that,s Uncle Williams Aunt Jane

Christmas

It is christmas again at the old cottage Home
  There is Bustle arround the old Hearth
The children again are Beginning to come
  To Join in its Pleasure and mirth
The Tables are loaded with food of the best
  And Each one seems filled with delight
But a shadow comes over our mirth as we think
  of the Chair that is Vacant to night

In the years that are past when the Hollidays came
  The children have always been Near
To Join in the sports at the old cottage Home
  And partake of its mirth and good chur

But we Hope when another Bright Christmas shall come
They will all be Toyather once more
Beneath the old Roof of the old Cottage Home.
Where so oft they have gathered before.
To Enjoy all the pleasures the Holledays give
That our Hearts may be Happy and bright
May no Shadow come over our thoughts when we think
That no chairs will be Vacant tonight

Five Faces on the Wall

I see on the ceiling Five Faces Toyather
They all that is Left of the sons of our Mothers
And as Time Flies away but a few years at best
Ere they all in the grave for a season must Rest

In the Kingdom of god they Have Joiled many years
And shared in its Blessings its sorrows and fears
With the Prophet of god they Battled for Truth
And Defended His name since the days of their youth

They Have stood by His side when the Battle was strong
And have Fought for the truth gainst oppression and wrong
Till they saw him laid low in the Cold silent grave
And they knew that His Heart was true loyal and Brave

And they knew that the Hands that were stained with His Blood
Had willfully Murdered a Prophet of god
And they knew Like a Lamb to the Slaughter He went
For warning all men of their Sins to Repent

And through life they have followed the Precepts He taught
Until age has come on and lifes Battles are fought
Still they Know that His words Have been True and Sincere
And they Ever's will cherish His memory dear

In the years that Remain may they feel no Regret
But be firm in the cause untill lifes sun shall set
When their mission is Filled may they meet them again
In a far better land Free from Sorrow and Pain

Prayer

Oh thou Mighty God of Jacob
   Listen to my Fervant Prayer
As I Bow the Knee before thee
   Wilt thou take me in Thy care
Wilt thou Grant me my petition
   I will ask thee not for wealth
But Instead Oh Father give me
   The Rich Blessing Life and Health
I ask not for worldly Honor
   I ask not for worldly Fame
But Instead Oh Father give me
   With they Children a good name
I will ask thee not for power
   I will ask the not for Might
But Instead oh give me wisdom
   To Direct me always right
Help me in my Duty Labor
   To Provide For Every need
And inspire my Heart to serve thee
   And thy ways and Counsels Heed
When my mission Here is finished
   And my Earthly labor

Take me back into thy presence
    There to Dwell For ever more
This we ask through Christ our succour
    Who our Sins and Sorrows Bore
And Ill come to the Honor
    And the glory Ever more

Persecution

How often the saints Have been Plundered and Mobbed
How oft they've been Driven and Plundered Robbed
How oft they've been Driven from Houses and Home
And left like the Beast on the Desert to Roam

How often their Blood Has been Spilt on the soil
How oft they've been Robbed of the fruits of their toil
How oft Their Homes Have been Burned to the ground
And their wives and their Children all scattered around

How often their path Has been marked by their Blood
As they fled from their foes over the cold Frozen soil
How oft by the way side the young and the old
Have sunk Down Exausted with Hunger and cold

They Have murdered the prophet and Patriarch too
They have Burned Down their Temple their cities had Fire
And the Saints Have been Exiled from Country and Home
Far out on the Mountains to find a new Home
    and liberty to Roam

Far away from their foes in the Deep mountain Dell
They have found them a home with the savage to Dwell
Where the Howl of the wolf and the growl of the Bear
Is wont to be mingled with Praises and Prayer

In the tops of the mountains away from their foes

The Lady of the Period

She meets a lady on the street good morning Mrs S
It seems an age since last we met Oh what a Splendid Dress
Tis green the very shade I love Oh what a splendid fit
Prey Tell me where you got the goods I must have one like it

She passes on the next she meets is Dearest Mrs J
Oh Dear I'm glad we meet again pray How are you today
Oh what a lovely Dress my Dear Did you meet Mrs S
I met Her just a moment since in such a Horrid Dress

In such a suit upon the street I never would be seen
The style and fashion ages old and would you think it green
And thus she flatters all she meets with Vanity and lies
When out of sight the next she meets the last shall criticize

But when at Home the scene has changed Extravagance and Dress
With Pride and Fashion has consumed Domestic Happiness
Now if such women still must move in good society
Good Honest wives will soon become a thing that used to be

Where we can go and Dwell in peace
From Noise and Bustle Free
Where you can Raise your little ones
In wisdoms Pleasant ways
And I in peace and Quietude
Can Finish up my Days
You know Im Growing old my Boys
And Soon must Pass away
Then Let me Live a Quiet Life
The Few years I may Stay
And when my Earthly work is Done
And all my Labors o,er
Ill Leave a Fathers Blessing Boys
If I can do no more
I want a little Fertile Land
Its acres may be Few
Enough to Raise my Dayly Bread
That I must surely Do
For I must Labor For my Bread
While Life and Health Remain
I will not Live By Charity
While Toil my wants will Gain
I want my Children Living Near
Their Faces I must see
For Life would Have but little Joy
If they were Far From
For when Im called From Earth away
To Take my Final Rest
I know they,d Lay me gently Down
With Flowers upon my Breast

Pride and Hautiness

And see How by Fashion the saints went astray.
    And Leaving their former position
No Doubt He would say as He oft Did of old
That fashions and Pride were more Potent than gold
In Lureing the saints from the true Shepherds fold
    And Leading them Down to Perdition

He Had told us before He would Tell us again
We should not be Haughty nor should not be Vain.
Our Dress should be Homespun Neat Tidy and Plain.
    For this was the Fashion in Heaven
He would say I have warned you against Fashion and Pr[ide]
So Teach you the will of the Lord I have Tried
But His Councils and Precepts you would not abide
    Although for your wellfare i was Given.

He had told us that Haughtiness led us to sin
And Vanity to it was very near Kin
And would lead from the path that the saints (walk in) shoued
    But you would not attend to the warning —
That if you His Council Refuse to abide
And Cling to your Vanity Folly and Pride —
In Glory you Never would sit By His side
    When we arise in that Bright Happy Morning

He would say If we followed the Precepts He Taught
Our pride Cast away us a Good Christian ought
And live and be saints till lifes Battles were fought
    We then a Bright crown would Inherit
We would meet Him again when our work Here was [done]
When our Mission was Finished our Victory won.
In that Bright Happy Home with the Father and Son
    And the saints who were led by His Spirit

Freedom and Liberty

Thank God there are True Noble men in this land
By the Old Constitution who firmly will stand
Brave Chieftains of Battle for Freedom and Right
In the strife gainst Oppression who Bravely will fight

Fight on Valiant Heroes thy names will be spread
On our Historys Page with the Heroes who Bled
And fought for our Liberty Freedom and Right
When the Old Constitution was framed in its might

They cause is a Just one the poor and oppressed
Will Remember the Names of Brown Morgan and Vest
In the Halls of our Congress who feared not to face
The Oppressor who Dared the Old flag to Disgrace

Then Hurrah for the Banner unfurl it on High
Set it Float on the Breeze while we send up the cry
For Freedom and Liberty over the land
While the Old Constitution unsullied shall stand

Deseret

Deseret Deseret Tis' our own Mountain Home
Where the saints from all Nations and Countries will come
Where the first to be caught in the Parable Net
We are all Here together in fair Deseret

We are Here from all Nations all countries and clime
For we plainly can see By the Signs of the Times
That the Joy Tree Has Blossomed the names is Set
We are waiting His coming in fair Deseret

From settlement County and State we have been Driven
We Have asked for Redress but no hearing was given

To plan our Destruction in Council they've set.
Ere we come to the Valleys of Thine Deseret.

But we, as we have Resolved with an Eye to the Spoil
To Possess all we've gained by our Labor and Toil
They, our Rulers with Falsehoods and Lies Have beset.
To Disfranchise the Saints in our fair Deseret

But God at the Helm will Direct us aright.
He will trust to H's arm through the Dark Stormy night.
We have faith in His Promise we I trust to Him yet
He will steer us safe through in our Fair Deseret

To E—

Can we forget The Friends we Loved
    In youths unclouded Hours
The Forms that wandered by our side
    In Pleasures sunny Bowers
Oh no let time and Change speed on
    To Tempt us to Forget
Still will those Bright and Sunny Days
    Live in our Memory yet

Can we forget The Happy Smile
    That gladdened our young Hearts
That almost Seemed to take away
    The Point of Sorrows Darts
Oh no Let absence Break the Wreath
    That Intercourse has twined
But never can it Blunt the Gem
    Of Friendship from the mind.

Can we forget The Eye that shed
   With us the parting tears
Oh no Let other friends Press Round
   To tempt us to forget
Our only answer to them is
   We must Remember yet

The Twin Graves

So Lowly were laid them beneath the cold clay
The Friends we have cherished in lifes early Day
In one Silent grave we have left them to sleep
They Have left us in sorrow and sadness to weep

Oh how Heavy our Hearts as we turned from the place
What sorrow was Pictured On Each Friendly face
The Tears fell in torrents from Hearts Running oer
As we left those Dear friends to be with them no more

Oh How we shall miss them around the lone Hearth
When we mingle our voices in Pleasure and mirth
In the Shadows of Evening at Parties and Ball
We shall think of those loved ones and tears Drops will fall

Yes sadly we.l miss them when in the gay throng
We Join in the Pleasure of Dance and of Song
Their memory we.l Cherish till lifes Dream is oer
And we meet past the shadows to part Nevermore

On the Death of my Daughter

Adieu my Dear Daughter adieu for awhile
We shall soon meet again if kind providence should
Then our sorrows will cease on that Bright sunny shore
With our friends and our Kindred whose gone on before

Shes Resting in Her lowly Bed
  Shes free from sorrow toil and Care
But Tears of sorrow oft is shed
  For Her who sleeps so sweetly there

Sleep on Dear Mother Take thy Rest
  Thy work on Earth is Nobly Done
Thy Spirit Now is with The Blest
  Where other Dear loved Friends are gone

Thy Children who are Left behind
  Still mourn The loss of one so Dear
So loving Faithfull True and Kind
  How Can we Help but Shed a Tear

But we must Toil a few more years
  On this cold Earth its Storms to Brave
But we Remember oft with Tears
  These simple words Our Mothers Grave

Who shared my sorrows and my joys
   She was my Happy Bride

Our Hearts were full of Love and Hope
   For Joy in years to come
We Braved the trials in our path
   Around our cottage Home
How swiftly Passed those Happy Days
   So full of Joy to me
Without a thought that since would bring
   Such Bitter misery

How fondly did I Hope that Fate
   When lifes Declining should come
Would leave us Calmly to Enjoy
   A Peacefull Quiet Home
But Such is life and such my fate
   Again I'm left to Roam
And Brave This Cold and Bitter world
   With Nither friends or Home

Deserted Friendless and alone
   In lifes Declining years
To Battle with the worlds cold scorn
   In sorrow and in fears
But come what will I'll Battle on —
   And Every Danger Brave
So will no Friends and Home again
   To lay me in my Grave

To Ada

We have laid Her away in the cold silent tomb
And our Hearts are overshadowed with sadness and gloom

But we know that the angels have taken her home
Where sickness and sorrow can Nevermore come
She is free from Temptation She now is at Rest
And god in His wisdom Has Done for the Best

How sadly we miss Her arround the dear Hearth
Her smile and Her laughter Her prattle and mirth
Her Raiment Her toys Her Companions and all
They will often Remind us and Sad tears will fall

And then at the table How lonely she'll be
There Her sweet little face we shall Nevermore See
The Bed where she slumbered the Pillow She Prest
And the Prayer that she murmured Retiring to Rest

But god in His wisdom has called Her away
Then why should we murmer or wish her to stay
In this cold dreary world full of sorrow and Pain
When we know that Ere long we shall meet Her again

My 59th Birth Day
And can it Be So many years
    Have Realy Past away
That I am Fifty nine years old
    On this my Natal Day
    That age is Realy Coming on
    And life is nearly Over
That all my Boyhood years are gone
    to come to me no more

I feel The same Impulses still
  The Sorrow and the Joy
The Hope of Happiness and Jore
  As when I was a Boy
But then The Labor and The toil
  My Limbs will not perform
My sight is Dim my Hearing Dull
  My Brow with Furrows worn

My Body Bent my Dark Brown Hair
  Is silvered oer with grey
All Tell me I am growing old
  All Tokens of Decay
Then when from Earth I m called away
  May Friends be gathered near,
To lay me Calmly in the grave.
  And shed the parting tear

Sad Memories
They Have Flattered Her pride and Her Vanity too
They have made Her Believe I am False and untrue
They Have filled Her with Lies till Her Love Her grave e
She Has left me alone when I m feeble and old

How well I Remember the Days of our youth
When she Seemed to be all that was Honor and true
Then Her love to my Heart was more Precious then gold
It Has Faded away when I m feeble and old

She has met other faces more youthfull and fair
Who will Flatter Her Pride and Her Vanity Share
They Have Lured Her away with the glitter of gold
She Has left me Because I am feeble and old.

Oh How Sad is my Heart as I sit Here alone
And I think of the years that forever are gone
When a Dear loving wife in my arms I could fold
Now she spurns me Because I am feeble and old

Altho fickle and false She Has been a good wife
And the Mother of those I love Dearer than life
for the Sake of those loved ones may Blessings unfold
Around Her who spurns me Because I am old

Sadness

My thoughts are Very Sad to night
  My Heart is filled with woe
Im thinking of the years gone By
  And tears of sorrow flow
Im thinking of The Dreary past
  Its sorrow and its pain
And feel the sun upon my Heart
  Will Never shine again

The Dreary past the present gloom
  The future none may see
But no Bright Prospect Hovers Round
  To Lend a Hope to me
No Home No friends to speak kind words
  To make me Hope again
Or feel the sun upon my Heart
  Will Ever shine again

There Free From all my Earthly Cares
  My Sorrow and my Pain
Perhaps upon my weary Heart
  The sun may Shine again

   Twenty Years ago
Oh give me back the good old times
  Of Twenty years ago
With all the Trials and the Toils
  We then Did undergo
But with it Bring the Joy and Peace
  With which we all were Blest
And Best of all the Sweet content
  That filled Each throbbing Breast

How Cheerfully Each day we toiled
  Our Daily Bread to Earn
Well knowing that a faithful wife
  Awaited our Return
No pride or Fashion to Destroy
  Domestic Happiness
Or Teach us Selfishness and Vice
  But all was Joy and Peace.

Our wives with willing Hands Did Toil
  Their Homespun to provide
To cloth their children and Themselves
  And all were satisfied.
Although no Dainties Decked our Board
  We Relished well our Food
Twas what the Earth Brings Forth to us
  And all pronounced it good

How happy were our Evenings spent —
    At parties or at Balls
Where not a Fit of Discontent
    Was known within the Hall
But Pleasure Beamed in Every Eye
    And Joy Filled Every Heart
And often would the Dawn appear .
    Ere we would cheery to part.   .

Then give Me back those Happy Days
    Though Hardships may betide
And take away Base Fashions Rule
    With Haughtiness and Pride.
A cheerfull Home with social Friends
    Though Poor that Home may be.
Tis Better Far than Pride and Gold.
    That Brings but Misery.

Hope

One by one they all are Leaving
    To a Southern Land they Go
They are leaving Me in Sorrow
    In this Land of Frost and Snow
Oh How Gladly would I Mingle
    With My Friends and Join this Band
Who are Leaving This cold country
    For a Brighter Sunny Land .

When I've finished up my Mission
    Neath the Fig Trees pleasant shade

Although Trials now beset me
    I Have Faith that God is Just
And will Bear me Safely through them
    If His Promises I Trust
And the Clouds that Hang above me
    And overshadow me to day
Will be Rifted and the Sunlight
    Will again Shine on our way

For the Spirit whispers to me
    That my Labor is not Done
I must Finish up my Mission
    Which is only Just begun
Although Years are Growing on me
    There are Better Days for me
Ere I lay me Down to slumber
    I shall fill my Destiny

Spring (a Burlesque)
A Thought has Struck me Just the thing
I'll Jot it Down my Pencil Bring
(Oh Dear what noise is that without)
(Now Charley what are you about)

Oh Glorious Spring thy Buds and Flowers
Thy Golden Sunshine and thy Flowers
(Thy gentle Zephyrs what a Riot
Now children cant you Keep more Quiet

Thy Meadows Green (There Minnie see
If some one is not calling thee)

Thy Meadows Green thy Fragrant air
Thy Sparkling Dew like Diamonds Rare
The Warbling of the Thrush and Linnet
(Ile cut some wood in just a minute)

Oh How I love thee Beauteous Spring
Thy Praises all the Poets Sing
The Brightest season of the year
(Go To the Office I be there)

I love to wander o'er the Hills,
And listen To the murmuring Rills
And cull the Flowers upon the plain
(There I must go I hear the train)

Friends.

Oh No I cannot live alone
   I must Have others Near me.
To pass the lonely hours away
   To comfort and to cheer me
Without Companions life would be
   A Desert lone and Dreary
Id Have a wife to comfort me
   When I am sad and Dreary

To be my one and loving Friend
   Though sorrow may betide me
And when we'd Reached the others End
   Id have Her laid beside me
Id Have a Peaceful quiet Home
   Where friends might sometimes gather

To Pass a social Holliday
    In Happiness togather.

I,d Have my Kindred living near
    Where I could often greet them
And When the Hollidays come Round
    With pleasure I would meet them
I,d Have them Gather Round my Board
    All in their Propper Places
Pertaking of my Humbell Fare
    With cheerfull Happy Faces

A few good Neighbors I would Have
A Man may sometimes Need them
For when the poor are in our midst
They,d Help to Clothe and Feed them
I,d have Enough of Worldly goods
Obtained by Honest Labor
To Keep us all from Knowing Want
Myself my Friend my Neighbor

Deseret

Oh what a sad Dilemma
    All the people Now are in
About the Mormon Institution
    Called the Barberism Turis
They seem to be Determined Now
    To Wipes us Out and set
The poor Deluded Mormon wives
    All free in Deseret

So in the Halls of Congress
    Over which our Banner waves

They have Robbed us of our Freedom
    And have Voted us all slaves
They Robbed us of our Franchise
    And Rulers over us Set
To Bring us into slavery
    In lovely Deseret

They have Robbed us of our Liberty
    They've Robbed us of our wives
They've Robbed us of our children too
    All Dearer than our Lives
And all for our Religion too
    That we such treatment get
While we are peacefull citizens
    Of lovely Deseret

They Drove us from our Settlements
    They Robbed us of our Homes
They Drove us from the Country too
    New Desert sands to Roam
Then from the State they Drove us
    No favor could we get
We wandered to the vallies of
    The lovely Deseret

Here we dwelt in peace a season
    Where by labor and by Toil
We have Built up Towns and Cities
    And Reclaimed the sterile soil
And the Lord has Blest us greatly
    Since our Religion here we set
In the peace He had Prepared for us
    The Vales of Deseret —

But our Foes are now Determined
They will Drive us once again
And Dispoil us of our Riches
And Possess our Fair Demain
So to Drive us From the Nation
They our Rulers have beset
But the Lord will not Forsake us
In our lovely Deseret

Religeon

There's a sort of Religeon some people Profess
They put it on Sunday when they go to Dress
And at night they will fold it and put it away
And they see it no more till the Next Sabbath Day
For such a Religeon I have not a Care
Give me a Religeon for Every Day wear
They will sit in the church with an Innocent look
While they Hear the good Doctrine contained in the Book
With their grave solumn Face you would think them so (Pure
That a Bad thought or action they could not Endure
Chorus
They will give you good Counsel and warn you from sin
And Tell you the way that a Saint should walk in
They will wear a long face through the whole Sabbath Day
And sometimes in meeting they'l Preach & they'l pray
Chorus
On Monday you'd see them go out on the street
To Take the advantage of Each one they meet
If it costs them a lie They will make a good trade
And they'l Boast of what they have Dishonestly made
Chorus
Sometimes you may see them around the Saloon
Or Down on the Store Steps from Morning till Noon

If they owe you theyl give you good promise for Pay
But you cannot depend on a word they will say
Chorus

In Tale and Gossip they sometimes Excell
And Flattery too and Make Mischief as well.
Thus Each Day in the week they their Time pass away
But theyl wear their Religeon on Each Sabbath Day
Its only a sham to say at the best
When they attire on Sunday in a Religious dress.

Home Agin

Well Here I am again at Home
And in My Quarters all alone
And must again my Toil Begin
By which my Dayly Bread I win

The Days since From my Home I went
Quite pleasantly have all been Spent
In Social Converse and good Cheer
By social Friends and children Dear

And then the little children too
How well they tried what they Could do
To Entertain us and to make
The Time Pass pleasant for our sake

Beneath our window they did sing
And make the air with Music Ring
Their childish laugh their merry glee
All made a Happy Time for me

But Happy Days Must have an End
And friend Must some time part with friend
To Battle with the cares of life
And share its Sorrows and its strife.

And so again with Heavy Heart
I must again Resume my part
And fill my Mission here below—
For soon Tis be my Turn to go

Farewell to my Home

Farewell to my once Happy Home
Farewell to the Cottage and Vine
   And the orchards Deep shade
    Where the children have Played
In the years when Content ment was mine

Farewell to my once loving Friends
Farewell to my children so Dear
     And the wife of my Heart
     I must now with Her part
Though it causes me many a Tear

Farewell to Each Token so Dear
I see them wherever I go
     That Reminds of the past
     And in Memory will last
And cause Tears of sorrow to Flow

Far down in the Journey of life
An outcast from Friends and from Home
     With a sad bursting Tear
     I must Leave all so Dear
And finish my journey alone

Oh how sad has life been in the past
And the future no Brighter may be
     With no Hopes sunny Ray
     To Illume my Dark day

Oh shed its effulgence in Me

The years are fast passing away
That Hastens her on to the Tomb
  Where I Hope to find Rest
    In the Land of the Blest
Far away from Earths Sorrow and Gloom

To my sister Esther   Feb 1894

Dear Sister you.ar Noticed My Letters of late
Have savored of sorrow and Trouble
It seems in this life the caprices of Fate
Have caused all my sorrows to Double.
My wife She that should be My comfort and stay
As we Pass through the shadows of life
She Has gone from Her Home She Has Left me for aye
My Darling My Dear cherished wife
No pen can my feeling of sorrow portray
My Little ones sit on my Knee
Ask where is my Mother who is she away
I wonder where Mother can be
The Tears Blind my Eyes as I try to impart
A shadow of what I Endure
Despair Grief and Sorrow Enshrouding my Heart
To me she was Spotless and Pure
For Twenty four years we Have traveled to gather
Through the Shadow and sunshine of life
Many storms we Have seen mixed with Bright sun (wreathe
She was always my own cherished wife
But his first and the worst Tie that Bound us is Broken
Bitter grief and despair fills my Heart
Those Hard Bitter words were so cruely spoken
Since News can Heal up the smart

this and the following was written in answer to Her letters to me

We must part and Forever Oh Hard is the Fate
That Tells of the wrongs I Endure
I cannot accuse Her Though Hartless and Frail
She once was so spotless and Pure
Yours Letter so kind to my Heart is a Ray
Of sunshine mid Darkness and gloom
For to Know I've a Friend on my Dark lonely way
As I pass to the Shadowy Tomb
To answer your Letter I'd surely be glad
But I feel so unfited to day
My mind is Too gloomy my Heart is too sad
To Tell you the Half I would Say
My Health is no better than when I wrote last
The children are able to go
I'm sure I cant Tell when our writes be past
The Ground is all covered with snow
Of the Question you asked I but little can Tell
I E said but little about it
I have Faith in the future that all will be well
I never a moment can Doubt it
Of the order of Enoch But little I Know
And Trouble I never will Borrow
For it comes fast Enough in this Life as we go
In to me Tis all trouble and sorrow

     To My Sister Esther

Dear sister you wish me to Tell you my mind
Of the order of Enoch but I Dont feel Inclined
To say much about it so little I Know
That on the grave subject no light could I throw
I E in his Letter said little to me
And all I could Tell is worth Nothing to thee
Besides I've concluded no Trouble to Borrow
For I find in this world Enough trouble and sorrow

What Earline thinks I am sure I can't tell
But Her thoughts and my own do not correspond well
But Earline you shall know of the trouble I've had
Though to night you cannot for my Heart is too sad
But this much you shall know she has gone to her mother
And caused me such anguish that time cannot smother
Oh How I would like to be with you awhile
To chase away sorrow Dull care to beguile
If seeds will be to you of any avail
Send to me your orders I'll send them by mail
If you have a needle or two you can spare
I should like Number 5 if less Sir I don't care
For the Old weed Machine And will send them to me
You cannot Imagine How glad I would be
For a paper I have not the money to send
And we have not a needle to match or to mend
In a very few days I'd send moneys for those
And then you shall take what you sent me before
Do not Bother about them if you have not them got
I will do Very well if I have them if not
My Health is not good as I said in my letter
And trouble and sorrow wont make it much better
But I think if I weather it through for awhile
I will make you a Visit Dull care to beguile
The children are with me at present & all well
But How long I shall keep them I am Sure I can't tell
I will Hope for the best For the worst ill prepare
If they too should leave me who then would care
This life is all filled up with sorrow and trouble
And in dealing it out they give ills and my double
The grave will soon End it and why should I care
When all of its pleasure for me is shewn Bare
The winter out here has been very cold
The cattle are Dying off both young and old

Your small Bundle cow has been found with the Rest
Joe lost two or three Horses one of them my best
There are Hosts of them already Dead on the Range
But the snow is fast leaving, I think it will change
Bright spring will soon be Here to make us all glad
But what is Bright spring time to Hearts that are sad
From spring Jake Ive not Heard for many a Day
If the D Ts are there I am sure I cant say
I never Hear from them whereas they are
Like others for me they seem nothing to care
I much Doubt if to any ... well it could come
I should Very much like to if I could leave Hen
Yes Milas is Married and got Him a wife
And He thinks He Has got all He wants in this life
I Believe youve not seen Her Allice adkins Hers name
But I Hope She's a Very good girl all the same
When Millie will marry I am sure I cant say
There is plenty of time yet for many a Day
Her and Laura Keeps House for the children and me
But How long it will be so Tis Hard now to see
But as Everything changes so This will of course
Like Everything Else Change For Better or worse
Although Heard is my lot for my Children I Bear
For they certainly Need all a Parents fond care
You liked the Envelope I sent you before
When I can Think of it Ill send you some more
The stamps that you sent me are money to me
For I send Them for Seeds and Envelopes you see
But youd fas better keep them than give them away
For I now see no Prospect I Ever can pay
By the mail, all the seeds that you want will be sent
If your Neigbors will Buy they Send for what you want
So now I will close wishing you a good night
And Hoping you soon sue a letter will ...

But Too Hard in your Thoughts dont to Evelien be
For surely he Has he is a good wife to me

            On The Death of My Brother Joel
No No Not Dead but gone to Sleep
     Ere long to wake again
When christ Shall Come again to Earth
     A Thousand years to Reign
Not Dead but Resting for awhile
     From all the Soils of Earth
To Quicken in a better Home
     And gain Celestial Birth

Not Dead but waiting in the grave
     A Brighter crown to wear
To mingle with His Early Friends
     Their Happiness to share
He is not Dead To Realms above
     His Spirit Free Has Fled
No more to Mingle with us Here
     But Say not He is Dead

He is not Dead it Cannot be
     His Labor Has been Vain
That He is Dead and in His grave
     To never Rise again
No He Has Passed behind the Veil
     To meet His Friends who Bled
And Died as Martyrs for the truth
     No No He is not Dead

            Reflection.   1880
I ae wandred over the Road again
     I ve Traveled oft Before

In years gone Bye and Marked Each Spot
  I Knew in Days of yore
(Virgin Spring) Twas Here with wife and Children to
  I Camped one Dreary night
But never Thought of Loneliness
  To me the world was Bright
(Rocky Ridle) And Here again I Camped one Night
  When Sickness Racked my Frame
But I in youth and full of Hope
(Santaquin) Could Bravely Bear the Pain
And Here in youths Bright sunny Day
  I Reared my lowly Cot
And many Happy Hours I'v spent
  On this Dear Hallowed Spot
(Spring Creek) And Here again in later years
  I made my Humble Home
But Sorrow came and Closed arond
  And filled my Heart with gloom
(Payson) And Here again long years ago
  From Savage Hands to flee
I Found a Home to Dwell awhile
  My Children wifes and me
(Spanish Fork) My Noble Steed Had swam the Stream
  And I was safely oer
My wife and Children met me Here
  To See me Safe on Shore
And Here again was once my Home
  Twas Many years ago
Ere sorrows Pang Had Touched my Heart
  With Bitterness and woe

Of Days when I had Health and youth
    And Friends were Kind and true
And urbes in Virtue Love and Truth
    Were pure as Morning Dew
But now alone without a Home
    In Lifes Declining years
I often live those scenes again
    In Bitterness and Tears

Our Dear old Home

Our Dear old Home is Desolate
    As through Each Room I go
My Footsteps Cause a Hollow Sound
    Which Fills my Heart with woe
The Pictured walls I gaze upon
    Sad memories Bring to me
Of Happy Days forever gone
    And left But Misery

The Hall where in the Merry Danced
    To music Sweetest Streams
I've mingled oft with Social Friends
    I'll Never meet again
Tis growing Now a Shadow Deep
    Hangs O'er my Heavy Heart
It tells me with my Home and Friends
    I must forever part

And Darken Every Ray of Hope
    In Lifes uncertain Skies

Thus in The Evening of my Life
    Im Left without a home
Or loving Friends to comfort me
    An Still I must Roam
So I must Totter Down the Hill
    In Shadow and in Gloom
Until I Reach my Journeys End
    The Cold and Silent Tomb

        Christmas Again
At the old cottage Home it is Christmas again
And mirth and Enjoyment and Happiness Reign
With Hearts ourflowing with Pleasure and glee
They all are Delighted and Happy but me

With Food of the Choicest the Tables abound
And Dainties and Luxuries scattered around
With Sumptuous feasting and Rare Jolity
They all seem Enjoying the Pleasure but me

As the Shadows of Eve are begining to fall
They to finish Their sports Have Retired to the Hall
With Plenty of music of Rare melody
They all a Light hearted and Happy but me

I have toiled many years till Im weary and old
I have suffered the pangs of Thirst Hunger and cold
With the Hope that when age should come in there would be
A Home in this cold Dreary world left for me

But Fortune was Fickle and Friends were untrue
And my Hopes Have all Vanished away like the Dew
All the years that Remain I a wanderer must be
Thus No Home but the grave in this wide world for me

      May we Not Then Part as Friends

Since the golden Chain is Broken
      That once Bound us Heart to Heart
And the Cruel words are spoken
      That Has Severed us apart—
And our Paths are Now Diverging
      We Must live to Different Ends
We Must part Perhaps Forever
      May we not Then part as Friends

Many years we,ve shared togather
      All their Sorrows and their Tears
Now our Destiny Must sever
      In our Fast Declining years
Wrinkles Deepen on our Foreheads
      Silver Threads among the grey
Sight Grows Dim and Limbs Grow Feeble
      All are Tokens Of Decay

Showing that our years are Numbered
      That our Lives are Nearly over
Sadly Does the thought Come over me
      Must we part to meet no more
Life to me Has Little pleasure
      When with Friends I,ve Forced to Part
Must I Then Resign The Treasure
      That Has Wholly filled my Heart

Cruel Fate thy spell is Broken
    By what sorrow few can tell
Since the Cruel words are spoken
    Bravely will I say Farewell
But in coming years should sorrow
    Touch thy Heart and cause thee pain
When thy flattering Friends Desert thee
    Then perhaps we'll meet again

But I cannot spare this caution
    Heed it or 'twill cause Regret
Trust thy Summer Friends No longer
    Or thy Sun of Hope is set
When thy Brow becomes more wrinkled
    When thy Hair becomes more Grey
When thy Beauty Fades forever
    Summer Friends will fly away

To Charlotte

Dear sister this title to me is So Dear,
That I Hope you'l not Blame me for using it Here
For my Sisters and Brothers are Really So few
That I Hope I may still find a Sister in you

This title to me thou Hast Bone many years
I can only Resign it in sorrow and tears
Then one years that Remain let us love one another
At least with the Friendship of sisters and Brothers
                                                    / few

In this Hard Dreary world we have found Very
When adversity comes that will still Remain True
But may I still Find you a Friend to the last
A gem among Pebbles thy Lot has been Cast

My 66" Birth Day

Thanks Thanks Kind Friends For coming Here
     A while with us to stay
To Celebrate and Bring good cheer
     On this my Natal Day
You little Know How much of Joy
     Your Presence Here has Brought —
Or How good actions and kind words
     With Happiness is Fraught

When snow fills The Drooping Heart
     And gives the spirit pain
Kind gentle words may cheer us up
     And make us Hope again
Our Friends are few and life is Short
     Then Let us while we stay
With gentle words and kindly Deeds
     Bring Hope to all we may

Valentine,

Bright visions are passing before me to night.
Of the years past away That were Happy and Bright
And many Bright Faces before me appears
Of The friends of my youth That to me were so Dear
Oh How fondly I gaze on the scenes of the past
While Fancy allows the Bright vision to last
And I Hail those Bright forms as they pass from my View.
And the Brightest of all and most cherished was you —

All alone I must travel the Downhill of Life
With no Friend by my side with no Dear Johnny wife
For my Friends have all Vanished away Like The Dew
And now I am Shunned and Deserted By you

May God in His Mercy his Pity Bestow
As through the Dark shadow of Life I shall go
And Help me my Burdens and trials to Bear
And Provide me with Friends all my sorrows to share
And when I have Finished Lifes work here below
May I know Tis well Done and be Ready to go
Then among loving Friends who are Loyal and true
And the Dearest of all may I not them find you.

To Horace Edgar

Another Bud Has Drooped and Died
Ere it was in its Bloom
To Blossom in a Brighter Land
Beyond the Silent Tomb
Oh How we miss our Darling ones
With whom we've forced to part
To lay them in the Silent Tomb
Oh How it Rends The Heart

Oh How we miss their childish Forms
Around the lonely Hearth
Oh How we miss their Noisy sports
Their laughter and their Mirth
But we are Doomed to sorrow Here
While on the Earth we Stay
But yet we feel that God is just
He gives and takes away

on the Death of my grandson

We Shall Meet

We shall meet but we shall Miss Him
    There will be one Vacant Chair
When we gather Round the Fireside
    We shall Miss His Presence there
Just one year ago we Gathered
    In our Dear old cottage Home
Joy was Beaming in his Features
    And His Eyes with Lustre Shone

When we clasped the Hand at Parting
    Tears in Torrents Down ward Fell.
And our Hearts were filled with anguish
    As we said the Last Farewell
Now our little Band is Broken
    We are Drifting with the tide
And our Dear old Home Forsaken
    We are scattered Far and wide

We shall meet but Many Faces
    May be absent from our Band
They are Drifting from our circle
    They are Scattered through the Land
But we Hope once more to gather
    May each Broken Link be There
But Our Hearts will swell with anguish
    When we see the Vacant chair

        July 24th 1884
This is the Day we Celebrate
    In this our Mountain Home
For on this Day the Pioneers
    Into the Vallies Come

Just Thirty Seven years ago
    Our Banner was unfurled
On Ensign Peak our Loyalty
    To Show to all the world

On Each Succeeding year this Day
    We Have togathey Met
In Every Town to celebrate
    The Birth of Deseret
Then may our children yet unborn
    Still Celebrate with cheers
The Entrance in these Vallies of
    The Noble Pioneers

The [?]

Oh where are these Brave Valient Heroes
    Who stood By the prophet of god
And Valiently Fought in His service
    When Traitors were Seeking His Blood
Who wore out their Lives and their Fortunes
    Till they Saw Him Laid Low in the Tomb
And Still Have continued the warfare
    Though all was in Darkness and gloom

They are Lying along by the wayside
    Worn out by their Labor and Toil
They are Resting where Mobs and where Traitors
    No more can Rob Plunder and Spoil
They Have fought the good fight and have Finished
    Their Mission of Labor below
And now with the Martyrs before them
    They Dwell beyond Sorrow and woe

Oh how my Heart yearns For the Bright sunny Faces
All Beaming with Joy of my children and wife
And all those Dear Friends that Fond memory Entrales
So Dear to my Heart in the Morning of Life

How sadly I miss them as lonely I wander
Around my lone Cabin By night and by Day
And often in Twilight I silently ponder
Oer the Dreams of my Life in the Years past away

When all those Bright Faces were Hovering around me
And Favored by Fortune No sorrow I Knew —
But Dark Cruel Fate in its Fetters Has Bound me
And Forced me to Bid all Lifes Pleasures adieu

Now Friendless and Homeless all social Ties Broken
Alone I must pass through the Evining of Life
Till Death shall Relieve me and Banish Each Token
Of Love I Have borne For Friends Children and wife

To Terree   ... 13   1885

Dear Friend upon your natal Day
   With Joy we meet you Here
To show the Love we Bear for you
   And Join you in good cheer
Then may we Have a merry Time
   While we togather stay,
And when we part may Each one feel
   We.ve Spent a Happy Day
May Happiness Fill Every ~~Heart~~
   And Joy fill Every Heart
And Each one Feel a Willingness
   To act their proper Part

Let Every care be laid aside
  And Every Heart be light
And may no Jar or Discord come
  Our Happiness to Blight
And when we from Each other part
  May Each one Bear away
Remembrance of the Happy Scenes
  Of this your Natal Day

An Acrostic

To celebrate your Natal Day
  We all Have met you Here
Each Bent on passing off the Day
  In Pleasure and good cheer
Like children we have left our toil
  And thrown our cares away
In Mirth and Happiness and Joy
  To spend your Natal Day
Then Let us Have a merry time
  Let Every Heart be light
Here Let no Jars or Discord come
  Our Happiness to Blight
And when this scene shall come to part
  Let Every one Bear away
A fond Remembrance of the scenes
  Of this your natal Day
And of all sorrow care or strife
  Let mirth and Pleasure Reign
Each willing to Perform his part
  While we shall Here Remain
Relief our Motto and to you
  Our leader we will say
our Friends all join in wishing you
  Full many a glad Birth Day

To My old Coat

Thou Dear old Coat as Summers past
And winter Comes with storm and Blast
  I've Come for you again
For thou Has been my only Friend
On thee I always Could Depend
  Through winter Snow or Rain .

My Friendship has been Ever true
Since first I Bought thee Bright and New
  Fresh From the Tailors Hand .
And thou Hast served me many years
And Shared my sorrows Joys and Fears
  And always been my Friend

But We,re growing old and grey .
And soon we both will Pass away .
  But we will go Together
I'll Patch thee up and Brush thee too
And make thee Just as good as New
  To wear in Stormy weather .

Though thou art tattered old and Torn
I too am getting old and worn .
  Together we have Passed
Through many a Rough and Rugged way
And been companions many a day.
  And will be to the Last

Going Down the Hill

When I was young and in my prime
    With Nimble limbs and strong
But little sorrow then I knew
    For then my Heart was young
I Bravely toiled to win my Bread
    No matter good or ill
But Never Thought in those Bright Days
    Of going Down the Hill

I Battled Hard with poverty
    To Drive it from my Door
When sickness and when sorrow came
    Their pangs I Bravely Bore
With loving wife and children too
    My Humble cot to fill
And in my Joy I Never Thought
    Of going Down the Hill

But age came on and silver threads
    Were scattered Through my Hair
And many a furrow on my Brow
    Were marks of Toil and care
My Limbs grew feeble then my Heart —
    Began to feel a chill
For then I knew I'd Reached the Top
    And Turning Down the Hill

With feeble steps I tottered on
    But Fortune on me Frowned
My Dearest Friends Deserted me
    Like Fetters I was Bound
But Still I struggled with my Fate
    Faint weary worn and ill

With many a Jostle by the way
  In going Down the Hill

Now I am left without a home
  And Every Hope is gone
And over my Heart a shadow falls
  For I am left alone
A little more of woe my cup
  Of Bitterness to fill
I soon shall Drain its Dregs and Reach
  The Bottom of the Hill

Christmas Again 1885

Yes christmas is coming the Happy New year
Is swiftly approaching and soon will be Here
And Hearts not overburdened with sorrow and care
For mirth and Enjoyment begin to Prepare

For Joy and festivities Now are at Hand
And Feasting and Pleasure will Reign in the Land
And Every Enjoyment that wealth can Procure
Will be Shared in all Homes not too Humble or Poor

But are there not Hearts that are Heavy and sad
Whom the Hollidays will not make merry or glad
Where the Sting of Misfortune or sorrow or Pain
Or worn out and weary by Povertys Reign

Then let us be Brothers and Hunt out the poor
And with all the Needy Divide of our store
And cheer up the sorrowful Comfort the sad
And share with the Needy and make their Hearts gl

That none in our midst may have sorrow or grief
Where kind words or actions will give them Relief
That all may partake of our Mirth and good Cheer
A Bright Merry Christmas a Happy New Year

Christmas Eve   1885

Tis Christmas Eve and Every thing
    About the House is Still
Three little stockings on the wall
    For Santa Claus to fill.
Three children in the Trundle bed
    But cannot go to Sleep
So catch a glimpse of Santa Claus
    They from the covers peep

Ive told them that He would not come
    Till all within The House
Were Fast asleep and Every thing
    Is quiet as a Mouse
Tis Twelve o clock and now at last
    To Slumber they must yield
And Santa Claus has come and gone
    Their stockings all are filled

So in the Morning we shall hear
    Them shout with Noisy glee
For little makes such little ones
    As Happy as can be
So may we often Bear in mind
    That we may oft make glad
By little words or little Deeds
    A Heart care worn and sad

New Year   1885

Dear children on this New years Day
    My Thoughts are much of thee
And of the Friends in years gone bye
    That were so Dear to me
    When at thy Dear old Cottage House
    On Each Bright New years Day
We Met togather one and all
    To pass the time away
Where mirth and Music Dance and song
    Were Shared by one and all
And Every Heart was gay and bright
    In that Dear cottage Hall
But what a change our Little Band
    Were Drifting with the tide
A storm arose and wrecked our ship
    And we are Scattered wide
And some are in the Churchyard laid
    Beneath the Silent Clay
And others scattered over the Sand
    Or wandered far away
And never more our Little Band
    Will meet within the walls
For strangers pass its Petals now
    And Dances within the Halls
And if again we meet no more
    Beneath the Azure Skies
Oh may we meet in that Bright Home
    Where Storms Can Never Rise

        My "?" Birth Day   1885

We have all been togather yes all have been Here
We Have Passed off the Day in Joy mirth and good cheer

Now all have Departed and gone to their Homes
And again I am sitting Here Sad and alone
Tis my Birth Day I'm sixty two years old to day
All the Friends of my youth are fast passing away
Then why am I left Here to wander alone
In this cold Dreary world when its pleasures are gone

Seed Circular

Dear Friends and old Patrons Now listen to me
I've a few words to say which I think you'l agree
Will be good for us all in these very Hard times
And save for our Pockets a few Precious Dimes

In the years that are Past I have furnished you seed
For your farm or your garden as you have had need
And I've taken your Produce and trade for my Pay
But I've Most as yet Refused cash By the way

If I have by chance got a Dollar or two
The first Man would get it who called for His Due
And you in your turn might Receive it again
If in this Hard country you let it Remain

But if you send money for seeds to the East
You will see it no more in this country at least
And the seeds from the South are worth nothing at best
You will want in the money in them you Invest

But you'l do far the best with the seeds Raised at Home
Or Bro't from a climate as cold as our own
And let all the cash in this country Remain
And give us a chance to behold it again

With thanks for past favors in seasons gone bye
I will Hope in the future you'l get your sapply
From the seeds I send out or from me throng the mail
Or call it my place where I Keep them for sale

Stencil Circular

Now friends you've toiled the summer through
    To Raise a little grain
To Feed your wives and little ones
    When winter comes again
Now Dont be foolish as you've been
    And sell it at the store
Nor let the Miller steal it all
    As you Have Done before

But take a friends advice and mark
    Your sack, in letters plain
For from the Sacks you take to mill
    You'l Never see again
But if your name in letters plain
    Is printed on Each sack
If Theives should steal a sack of grain
    They'd surely Bring it Back

At Johnsons you can get your name
    In letters any size
I will do the job so neat and plain
    I will give you a Surprise
And when you want to go to mill
    You'l have to say no more
Good gracious all my sacks are gone
    Just as they were before

But here then are I so found them all
   The name is on them plain
These Things are worth their weight in gold
   In saving seeds and grain

    To Mother Curtis

Dear Friends we've met togather Here
   On this your Natal Day
To Join you in your mirth and Cheer
   And Pass the time away
Then let us lay our cares asside
   And children be again
Forget the many years gone bye
   Their Sorrows and their pain

Yes for a Day let us forget
   The snow flakes on our hair
Our weary limbs our farrewell Brow
   All marks of toil and care
Let us Forget the many scenes
   Of sorrow we have passed
Cold Hunger thirst Exposure to
   The cold and stormey Blast

Of sickness Death and all the pangs
   That filled our Eyes with Tears
In passing on our Journey through
   These long and weary years
Yes for a Day let all our cares
   And toil be laid away
Let mirth and joy Fill every Heart
   On this your Natal Day

Your Years gone Bye are Sixty three
    Just three times twenty one
Thrice you have Passed Majority
    And still your work not done
So may you Live for many Years
    And many Berth Days See
And Have more Joy at Eighty Four
    Than Now at Sixty three

Fortune

Oh what could Fortune offer me
    That I would Prise above
The Blessings of a Happy Home
    With these I Dearly Love
Whose sunny Smile would Chace away
    My sorrows Doubts and Fears
And Calm my Sad and weary Heart
    And wipe away my Tears
Whose gentle Voice of Melody
    Would drive away all Care
And make a Paradise on Earth
    For me with them to Share
Oh such a Home would be to me
    A Resting Place on Earth
From all the Sorrows and the Cares
    To which Each day gives Birth
I would Smooth my Pathway Down the Hill
    And Light me Through the Gloom
In passing on my Journey too
    The Dark and silent Tomb

Since first we met in Eastern lands
    And Vows of Friendship made
But coldness Dwells within they Heart
    A Cloud is on thy Brow
We Have been Friends together
    Why should we not be now

We Have been gay together
    Thou wert my Happy Bride
And Joy shone on thy features
    When we were side by side
But laughter now has fled thy lipps
    A gloom is on thy Brow
We Have been gay together
    Why should we not be now

We Have been sad together
    We've wept with Bitter Tears
Oer the silent grave where slumbered
    Our Hopes For future years
Those Voices Now so silent
    Should bid thee clear thy Brow
We Have been sad together
    But what should Part us Now

        Back again   1882
Yes I have wandered back again
    To that old Cabin Home
Where I have spent so many years
    Before Dark Sorrow come
Ive met my children and my Friends
    Who were so Dear to me
And her who in those Happy Days
    I loved so Tenderley

I've wandered through the orchard too
    I've stood within the Hall
I've gazed upon the pictures there
    Upon the parlor wall
I've marked each spot I knew so well
    In years long past away
I've lived again those Happy scenes
    Of youths Bright Sunny Day

The Ladys Pet   1882

He sits upon the store steps
    His cigarette to smoke
And talk His Silly Nonsense
    And pass His Vulgar joke
He stares at Every woman
    That passes through the Door
He whittles up the Boxes
    He finds arround the Store
He stands arround the corners
    He saunters up the street
To tattle and to gossip
    With Every one He meets
He saunters in the parlor
    He takes the Easy chair
He Flatters all the ladies
    And talks His Nonsense there
He whittles on the carpet
    And smokes His cigarette
He does not Deem it Vulgar
    He is the ladies Pet

The Last Rose in Autumn
Thou Beautiful flower why cannot thou Hither
When the cold wintry wind was abroad in the land

And the Frost on thy Petals will cause thee to shiver
And fall from thy Stem By its withering Hand
Oh No Ill not leave thee By cold winds to perish
So fondly Ill Pluck thee and Bear thee away
Thy Beauty and Fragrance So fondly Ill cherish
Till Thy Beauty shall fade and thy Fragrance Decay
Then art last of thy Race to my cabin I Bear thee
Thy Beauty shall fade in a Vace on the wall
And while thou Remainest thy presence shall cheer me
And thy Fragrance shall Float in my Bachelors Hall

Forty Year ago   1884
Im Sitting Here alone Dan
    In my old cabin Home
And Visions of the years gone byt
    Unbiden to me come
And many Faces I behold
    Of Friends you used to Know
When we were Boys togather Dan
    Just Forty year ago

Things are not as they were Then Dan
    Especially The Girls
They Did not wear their Pin backs then
    Their switches Borands or curls
Eight Homespun yards would make a Dress
    For those we used to Know
They Spun and wove and made it then
    Just Forty years ago

They Took their Music Lessons then
    upon The Spinning wheel
And Time was Measured by the Skeins
    And Knots upon the Reel

They Learned to Dance by Housework then
    And Kneading up the Dough
And Doing up the Kitchen work
    Just Forty years ago

They then were Fair and Healthy Ban
    And always Looked so Neat
And when we met at Spelling school
    Oh How our Hearts would Beat
For fear some other Fellow Dan
    Would Cut us out you Know
And Leave us on the Door step
    Just Forty years ago

But many years have past since then
    No more such girls we find
The girls we meet with Now a days
    Are of a Different Kind
They Look more like a wasp than silk
    The girls we used to Know
And take them Home from Spelling school
    Just Forty years ago

They Now wear Braids and Switches
    And Pin backs, Pads and Lace
They Squeese themselves so tightly
    They are Purple in the Face
They Dance all night at parties
    And Flirt with Every Beau
And think it Low to work like those
    Of Forty years ago

To Reach Down to the Carpet
    They get upon their Knees

They Burst their stays whenever
    They are obliged to Sneeze
They lounge upon the Sofa
    (Ma does the work you know
It was not so with those Dear girls
    Of Forty years ago

Then Dear Perhaps tis Better
    That we are growing old
And soon with our Companions
    Will gather to the fold
For were we young and Hansome
    How could we play the Beau
There's not one Left Like those Dear girls
    Of Forty years ago

To Alice

In the silent grave we have laid her away
So sweetly she slumbers Beneath the cold Clay
But many a Heart swells with sorrow and Gloom
When we think of the Dear one we've Laid in the tomb

How sadly we.l miss Her arround the old Home
Where the children are waiting for mother to come
No.more to Her bosom their forms will she press
No. more will they feel a fond Mothers Caress

Yes sadly we.l miss Her when in the gay throng
We mingle our Voices in Mirth and in song
At Meeting at Parties in Parlor or Hall
We shall think of the Dear one and tears Drops will Fall

But god in his wisdom has called her away
Then why should we murmur or wish Her to Stay

In this cold dreary world Full of sorrow and Pain
When we know that Ere long we shall meet Her again

The Hollidays   1889

The Hollidays again haue come
Annother year has passed and gone
And in its Tide has Borne away
The Friends I loved in childhoods Day

When I was young and but a boy
These Days I Hailed with childish Joy
But now they Bring but sighs and Tears
And Toll away the passing years

And of the few that's left to me
One more is in Eternity
They Bring grey Hair to me and Plow
The Furrows Deeper on my Brow

They Dim my sight my body bend
And warn me Life is near its End.
They Rob me of my Friends and Home
And Leave me Friendless and alone

Children and Friends

Dear children and Friends I must bid you adieu.
For a short time I now must be absent from you
There are other Dear Friends who are looking for me
And I am quite anxious their faces to see.

Those Dear little Children who love me so well
I shall think of them often wherever I Dwell
And Pray for their welfare wherever I Roam
Until I shall Return to the Dear ones at Home

May god in His Mercy Preserve us I Pray
Until I shall Return in some new Future Day
And keep us in safely Till Life shall be o,er
And we meet Past the shadows to Part No more

To the Missionaries

Brothes Joseph and Albert we meet with you here
Tis perhaps the Last Time for a long weary year
And we wish Him to say that when with you we Part
You still will retain a warm place in Each Heart

And although we with Pleasure shall bid you good Bye
Tis with Sad Heavy Hearts and with Tears in our Eye
And a Prayer to our Father to Keep you from All
While you shall be absent your Mission to fill

At morning and Evening whenever we Pray
We shall ask Him to Bless you where ever you stray
And Keep you from Sickness Temptation and pain
Until you Return to your loved ones again

And while you are absent Keep god for your Friend
And ask Him to guide you your cause to Defend
And Keep you away from Temptation and sin
And firm in the cause you are Laboring in

And when the time comes That your labor is Dun
May you Find Many Sheaves that your labor has won
And Return to your Home wives children and Friends
We shall meet you with Joy when your Pilgrimage Ends

To Joseph

Your letter was Duly Received my Dear Boy
And we all have Perused it with Pleasure and Joy

To write Best us the tidings you she had good Health
And we hope will Continue Tis better than wealth
Then there was the picture Oh what a surprise
We Have gazed on it fondly with Tears in our Eyes
And I almost Immagine tis going to say
Good Morning a you Father Howare you to day
I have shown it arround to your Friends one and all
And now it Hangs up in a Frame on the wall
And Ive Heard many Kindly Expressions to day
And some of them asked me to give it away
But as long as I live I shall Let it Hang there
With a few score of others I prize Very Dear
It will be but a Very short time till I go
Then the children will Share all my Keepsakes you Kno
Yous children and Anna Quite well have all been
I was Spending last Evening at Georges with them
And Don and Cecilia was also there Too
And we often were Thinking and Talking of you
All the Rest of Your Friends about Here are Quite well
But Amos with Frances has had a bad Spell
Of Diptheria But now she is getting all Right
So He said in a letter I got tother night
The aunts has been Very open till Now
I was thinking we soon Should be starting the plow
But tis cloudy tonight and I think it will storm
For the air out of Doors is Quite pleasant and warm
From Ossis and Millie I get not a word
They Had not Reached Iowa the last that I heard
But I think when they come I shall go with them Home
For Tis lonely to wear out the winter alone
But you all ride to me Here for I soon shall Return
For you know with my Seeds I a living must earn
And my mail will come to me wherever I be
I still look for your Letters so write them to me

There is nothing more now I can think of to writt
So will close up my letter and bid you good night.
With a Hope you may live to Return with much Joy.
When your mission is finished God Bless you my Boy

When with ours f.. .. .. f .. .. p.. t
When with ours Friends we are Forced to part
Oh How it Rends the Drooping Heart
But when we Know we Part Forever
Oh How it makes the Heart strong Sever.

Then may we not a Hope Maintain
That we ere long Shall meet again
To spend the few years of ours Life
Joyatther Free from ... and Strift

With Friends and Children while we Stay
That we in peace may Pass away
Well Knowing that ours work is Done
And Crowns of Glory we have won

Then give to me a word of cheer
To comfort me while I am Here
That we may meet some future Day
In Lands that now are far away

To Sunday School
Oh come my little Playmates
To sunday school away
To learn ours little Lessons
On this the sabbath Day
The sun is shining Brightly
The Dew is on the grass

Then let us off to Sunday School
    To join our little class
Say Bye your Toys and Marbles
    Your Play things put away
And cease from Play or Labor
    On this the Sabbath Day
We there shall meet our Playmate
    All Dressed so clean and neat
And there our loving Teachers
    With Happy faces greet
Then let us off to Sunday School
    And cease from work or Play
And Try to be good Children
    On this the Sabbath Day

The Old Mans Darling   1886

Would you be an old mans Darling
    Would you be his loving wife
Would you smooth His lonely pathway
    Down the Turbied Stream of life
Would you speak kind words of comfort
    Would you chase His cares away
Would you Try to love an old man
    Who is wrinkled old and grey
Would you do this your an angel
    I Have met along my way.
Who will fill my life with Sunshine
    Turn my Darkness into Day
Who will Drive away my sorrow
    Make my life a Sunny Dream
While Im passing through the Valley
    Down lifes Dark and Turbied stream
If your love is pure and Faithfull
    Till we pass beyond the Stream

Would you be an Old mans Darling
Or a young mans Humble Slave

(Gossiping)

Today I have been Thinking oer
The Mischief Done in Guessing
And think if I could Still my Thoughts
Perhaps Twould be a Blessing
For we are apt to make Remarks
That do not prove so pleasant
About imagenary Faults
Of those who are not present
And oftentimes an Idle word
That we Have Rashly Spoken
Has Injured some Dear Friend of ours
And Ties of friendship Broken
I guess that Mistres So and so
Is not what He should be
For I was Told the other Day
That Him and Mrs. C
Were Seen Togather at the gate
At Nine the other Night
And that would Indicate to me
That all things were not Right
And there is Mistres Whats His name
Who used to be so Poor
And now His getting Rich so fast
He owns one Half the store
And He has built him a new House.
Owns other property
I guess His Riches Has not all
Been got by Honesty
I wonder if Miss so and so
Thinks People Do not Know

What she went to the City for
   With Mister So and So
She Tried to Keep it all So still
   She thinks She.s Smart No Doubt
But Every body Knows it now
   The Gossips, found it out
Oh Dont Miss Jenkins put on airs
   And try to cut a Swell
You.d think to see Her on the street
   She Realy was a Belle
Of Twenty one But I am sure
   She.s Fifty five or more
I guess she aunts to catch a Beau
   A Fortune to Secure
Tis Very clear that old man J
   Is after Widow B
And He Expects She.l Marry Him
   But That must Never be
They say He.s got His Recomend
   I think it is a Shame
That Such a man Should Have a wife.
   The Bishop is to Blame
And then there is the Widow B
   Down on the other street
I see the old man there to-day
   They say They often meet
There must be Some thing wrong I am sure
   Some body ought to go
And see what Business He Has there
   And Let the people Know

   Is I my God

I am sitting Here a Thinking
   And the Question Comes to me

And Id Like to Have it answered Now
    If such a thing can be
Tis a thing of Great Importance
    And the question it is this
Is it any Bodys Business
    What anothers Business is

Is it any bodys Business
    If a man should wish to wed
And He calls upon a Lady
    With that Notion in His Head
And the Lady is Quite willing
    To Exept Him for a Beau
Is it any bodys Business
    But their own Id Like to Know

If a couple wish to Marry
    In the street or in the Hall
And they Call upon a Justice
    Both agreeing to it all
And He says the Ceramony
    That will change the two to one
Is it any bodys Business
    Please to tell Me But their own
When you go up Town some morning
    You might Hear some Shocking Tale
Of some Brother or some sister
    Who Had proven weak or Frail
Should you go about and tell it
    That the people all may Know
Or say not a word about it
    But I Hope it is not so

If a coal mine Has been opened
    And the owners all agree
On a price to sell the Coal at
    To the public you or me
And the coal is mined and lying there
    All Ready to be sold
Is it any bodys Business
    What the price is for the coal .

Should the Bishop Take a Notion
    Now and then to Have His way
Should we Rise and Fight against Him
    Or be passive and obey
While we Hold Him in position
    Should He Lead us or be Led
These are some of the great Questions
    That are Running in my Head .

There was a Time when Joseph
    Gave the Saints a little Key
And He said if they would Heed it
    It would Bring prosperity
It was Simply Mind your Business
    It was called the Mormon Creed .
But He,s gone Perhaps tis Better now .
    His Council not to Heed

He was Nothing but a Toyy
    Of a Very Early Day
With His precepts and his Councils
    We Have Nearly Done away
But the Question is before me
    Now to answer do not miss

Is it any bodys Business
    What anothers Business Is

If it is or if it is not
    I would Realy Like to Know
For I know that if it is not—
    There are some who make it so
For they gather on the corners
    And they Gossip Every where
Whether your Business is my Business
    Or whose Business it are

To David

Dear ~~Friends~~ we have gathered together to day
A Tribute of Love to our Brother to pay
Who will Leave us Ere long for a far distant Land
To Preach to the Nations as Christ did Command

Then Let us all Join and in unison pray
That God will Protect Him while He is away
And keep Him from Danger Temptation and Ill
While He shall be absent His Mission to fill

That the Spirit of God may attend him Each Day
As a Lamp to His Feet that will show him the way
And Enlighten his mind against Error to Fight
While He Preaches the Truth and contends for the Right—

Now we say to you Brother be Faithfull and true
And God will Protect you and see you safe through
He will Raise you up Friends if you trust to His arm
Who will shelter and Feed you and keep you from Harm

And in whatever Country or Land you may stray
Your Friends Here will Ever Remember to pray
For your Safety Prosperity Welfare and Life
Until you Return to Friends Children and Wife
And when you have Finished your Mission away
May we all meet again Neith this Roof as to day
And may Joy Peace and Happiness Ever attend
You while your away is the wish of your Friends

To David

We have mes you Here to night   Brother D.
For we Thought it would be Right Brother D
    Since it May be Many a Day
    Ere we Meet with you this way
But we shall for you Pray   Brother D.
That the Lord may be your guide Bro. D
And you may in him abide   Bro D
    May you Have the gift of Speech
    To Enable you to Teach
    And the word of god to Preach Bro. D
May you always Meet with Friends Bro D
Until your Mission Ends   Bro. D
    And when your work is Done
    May we meet Here Every one
    As we all this Day have Done Brother D
But while you are away   Brother D
Do not Fail to watch and Pray Brother D
    That the Lord your Mouth will fill
    And Preserve you from all Ill
    While you do His Holy will Brother D
May you many Converts gain   Brother D
While you absent Shall Remain Brother D
    But when the Time shall come
    To Return to Friends and Home
    May you know all is well Done Brother D

Retrospection

Before me the glass that my wrinkles Doth show
With comb cue and Wash stand and Basin Below
And above is a Motto Encased in a Band
A gift from my Daughters and made by Her Hand
Near Bye is the Cupboard I was made by Myself
With all sorts of Dishes arrayed on Each Shelf
Some were gifts from my friends Some were Bought at the store
An odd sort you would say were you looking them oer
Then there is the tin ware arrayed on the wall
The Bread board and Rolling pin Stone ware and all
And the old cooking stove Stands below on the floor
And the Bed in the corner stands near the Shop Door
At the foot is my Trunk which is filled to the Brim
With all sorts of Plunder all Roughty Stowed in
Then theres two or three chairs I beleive that is all
That makes up the Store of my Bachelors Hall.
Should you chance to step in and look over the place
You at once would Declare Tis a shame and Disgrace
In a country where women So plenty are seen
To live in a cabin So low and so mean
There is litters and Dirt Scattered over the Floor
And an old Dirty Towel Hangs up on the Door
And the Bed is not made and the fire has gone out
And the things in the Room are all scattered about
Every Dish on the Cupboard is covered with Dust
And the Knives Forks and Spoons are all Turnished with (Rust)
You would think it Had passed Through a Terable Squale
And Turned things Topsy Turvy in my Bachelors Hall
Oh why am I Doomed to Endure such a life
Oh where are those loved ones my children and wife
And where are the friends of my youths sunny Day
Like the Dew in the Sun they have Vanished away

But those who have Passed o,er the River of Time
They are calling to me from a Happier clime
Them why should I Finger But answer their call
And leave this cold world with my Bachelors Hall

Wishing

In trying to amuse Myself
  A subject wise or witty
I Sometimes try to study up
  To form a little Ditty
And in the Catalogue at last
  By Hunting and by Fishing
Ive Hit upon the Very thing
  The Harmless one of withing
And if by chance I get my wish
  I will better our Condition
And if I dont Iaill Do no Harm
  For theres No Harm in withing
I wish that people would be true
  And Kind to one another
And to Each other truly be
  A sister or a Brother
I wish that Happiness and love
  And Every Human passion
That Has its Orygin above
  Would come and Keep in fashion
I wish that pride and Vanity
  And Every low ambition
was Banished from the Human Race
  And lowered to perdition
I wish that people would not Speak
  So ill of one another
But always Speak a gentle word
  For sisters or for Br.

I wish there was no thieves to steal
    Or Rob a Friend or Neighbor
But always spend their time Instead
    In doing Honest Laber—
I wish that all who are so fond
    Of other people Teaching
Would take their own advice Themselves
    And Practice all their Preaching
I wish that people would not mind
    The Business of another
Or spend their time to Village
    And scandalize Each other
I wish that people who have wealth
    Would Help the poor and Needy
Instead of Hoarding up their gold
    So covetous and Greedy
I wish Religion could be worn
    On Saturday or Monday
Or any week day Just the same
    As it is worn on Sunday
I wish that people would not tell
    So many Lies in trading
But tell the Honest truth Instead
    Of Falsehoods So Degrading
I wish that Liquor was not used
    By Drunkards who abuse it
But only used as Medicine
    Or where we need to use it
I wish Tobacco was not Known
    To those who smoke and chew it
They would be wiser better men
    And Richer if they Knew it
I wish young men would spend their time
    In doing Honest Laber

Instead of going around the street
    Disturbing every Neighbor
I wish that women would not try
    To follow Every Fashion
And make themselves Rediculous
    By putting such Vile trash on
I wish they'd wear their Homespun now
    That gave them Health and Beauty
Forty Years ago Ere Fashions wiles
    Had led them from their Duty
I wish our wives were Honest true
    Kind gentle True and loving
Discarding Vile and Flattery
    Our Help meets truly proving
I wish that Husbands would be true
    Kind gentle and Forbearing
To wives and children Ever Kind
    Their Joys and sorrows Shareing
I wish that Children would Incline
    To Study and to Learning
Our good Examples proffit best
    Our Bad Examples Spurning
I wish we Had just gold Enough
    Obtained by Honest labor
To satisfy our Every want
    Ourselves our Friend our Neighbor

An Acrostic

Go Fill the Glorious Mission that god Has given thee
on though we Part in sorrow we with Prosperity
(n thee may all the Blessings that Heaven can Bestow
Repose while on thy Journey of Pilgrimage below
(o Bear with thee our Blessing and Prayer that thou mayest be
(n aided by His presence throughout thy Ministry

This was written for our
Pastor Rev George Scougless
when he left us on being
appointed to thy Synod of thy
funded apostles

Thy Name shall be Remembered when in our secret pray,
Each Evening and Each morning we seek protecting Care
Around thy Head Entwining may Happiness be Found
Secure from all Temptations may Joy and Peace abound
Dear Friend may life be Happy for many years to come
Ere thou art called to Leave it and find a better Home
Long may the good Examples and Precepts thou Hast given
Live in our Hearts to Help us to find our way to Heaven.

Is the old Home Lonely

Children is the old Home Lonely
    Since I've wandered far away
Is my Name some times Remembered
    When you Bow the Knee to pray
When you gather Round the fireside
    Is there then a Vacant Chair
Do you think of Him thats absent
    With a wish That He was There
When the Evening shadows gather
    And the Dayly Toil is o'er
Do you Listen for my Foot steps
    At the Dear old Cottage Door
Do you Think of me at Evening
    When Retireing to your bed
Do you ask of Him a Blessing
    On your wandering Fathers Head
Wandering o'er the Earth so Dreary
    Without Home or Friends to Love
Never more to Mingle with you
    Till we meet in Heaven above

A Lonely Christmas

Tis winter the Snow is fast Falling
    The Trees are all Bare of Their Leaves

246

The Beautifull Streams are all Frozen.
The Icicles Hang at The Eves
The christmas Bells Merily Ringing
Theirs Music and mirth in the air
The Tables are Sumptously loaded
With Dainties and Delicate Fare
All Friendless and Homeless I wander
Earths Pleasures No more to Enjoy
With No one to Share in my Evils
Excepting my Brave Hearted Boy
He Patiently Bears Cold and Hunger
But His Bravery. causes me Pain.
For I know that He thinks of His Mother
And longs to be with Her again
How sad is the change in my fortune
I once was Respected by all
When the Hollidays come there were Plenty
To gather in parlor and Hall.
And Plenty to Sit Round my Table
And plenty to Flatter and Smile
For feasting and Dancing were Frequent
And none were suspected of guile
When fortune Smiled Friends gathered Round me
So Trusting and loving and Kind
But when fortune frowned they all left me
Like chaff in the warm summer wind
But tis well for I now can discover
The Chaff has all gone with the wind
But the few grains of wheat that are with it
Is left in the garner behind

Musing

The Clock has Struck The Hour of one
And I am sitting Here alone

This and the following were written at The Residence of my son Apl 1883

The busy world is fast asleep
And Visions oer my fancy creep
The years long past away I seem
To live again in fancys dream
Again my childhood Home I see
Im sitting by my mothers knee
With father Sisters Brothers all
Are gathered in the Cottage Hall
Again the fields I wander oer
And cull the fragrant flowers once more
And in the orchard watch the Bee
And live the scenes of Infancy
The Vision changes year by year
The Prophet Josephs Voice I hear
Proclaiming to the world the News
First to the Gentiles then the Jews
That God again has set His Hand
To gather out from every land
The pure in Heart to do His will
In Latter Day work to fulfill
Oh what a scene now comes to view
The Patriarch and Prophet too
Within a Prison walls are cast
And Mobs Disguised are gathering fast
They charge and open Bursts the Door
It leaves them weltering in their Gore
Oh what a sight now meets my Gaze
Their Cherished Temple in a Blaze
Their cities all in Ruin Lie
And old and young are Forced to fly
Through summers sun and winters snow
The women children all must go
And leave their Homes and all behind
Far in the west a Home to find

Their food and clothing scant each day
And many perish by the way
A Brighter scene I now behold
Men women children young and old
Are Gathering in a Pleasant land.
Far from the Spoilers cruel Hand.
In peace they Dwell far from their foes
The Desert Blossoms like the Rose.
Large cities Now appear to View.
And Churches Halls and Temples Too.
W{.th} spreading farms and golden grain
And Orchards Scattered o'er the Plain
With peace and Plenty Joy and Health
And By Industry Stores of Wealth.
The Vision Changes once again
Their Foes Have Crossed the Desert, Plain
They are Reached this Peaceful Quiet Shore
And now are in our midst once more
They Try our Leaders to annoy
Our Farm and Peaceful Homes Destroy
To Rob us of our Fair Domain.
And Drive us from our Homes again
Oh Lord where Shall thy People go
To Serve thee In this world below
We still will Trust thine arm to Guide
For thou wilt Show us where to hide.

Paddle Your Own Canoe

Now Boys as I am growing old
  And soon Shall Pass away
I wish to say a word to you
  To Help you on your way
The Lessons I have learned through Life
  I wish to Leave to you

That they may help you when you try
    To Paddle your own canoe

In starting out in life my Boys
    Let Truth your watchword be
Let Virtue ever be your guide
    And Bear you company
Let Haughtiness be cast away
    And Pride and Envy too
And lay Hyprecisy aside
    And Paddle your own canoe

Let Slander Never pass your Lips
    Keep words of censure in
Speak Kindly to the Erring for
    You Know not why they Sin
For many a craft is wrecked and lost
    When sunlight peeps not through
In storms Kind words like sunlight Helps
    To Paddle your own canoe

Win many Friends though Trust but few
    Guard well the words you say
For you will many a Traitor find
    In Passing on your way
When words are spoken Carelessly
    They oft much Mischief do
Speak Kindly or Speak not at all
    But Paddle your own canoe

Should you be called to give advice
    Be carefull what you teach
Let it not Tend to gender strife
    But Practice what you preach

Plain simple Council kindly given
  With chosen words and few
Is better far than Flattery
  But Paddle your own canoe

Perhaps you say I did not Heed
  The Lessons I have Taught
Tis Very true and many Times
  They Dearly have been Bought
Tis what Experience has Taught
  Much good I will Bring to you
If you will Proffit by my words
  And Paddle your own canoe

My 61' Birth Day

How swiftly Glide the years away
That Bring about my Natal Day
Till Now they Tally Sixty one
And I am almost left alone

The Last so Very Short has been
And yet what sorrow I have seen
Of Brightest Hopes of Friends untrue
All Vanished like the morning Dew

In youth they passed so slowly bye
And now they almost seem to fly
And with their tide they Bear away
The Friends of youths Bright sunny Day

Far away among the Mountains.

Far away among the Mountains
    Where the wild winds whistle free
I have Reared my lowly Cabin
    For my little Boy and me
And we try to be Contented
    With our lonely Humble lot
While we try to Earn a living
    And to Beautify our cot
When we Rise from Bed Each morning
    He a Breakfast will prepare
For His four White Snowy Rabbits
    Which He tends with anxious Care
Then the chickens get their Rations
    And the two pigs in the pen
And our good old Faithfull Major
    Who our friend has always been
Then our gentle yellow ponies
    Must be fed and watered too
When we Rise from bed Each morning
    This is what we have to do
Then Maria calls to Breakfast
    We are Ready Him and me
This will close the morning service
    For our little Famaly
Soon one Breakfast we have finished
    I must to the Garden hie
While He Harnesses the Horses
    To the Harrow or the plow
Then I toil till I am weary
    For you know I'm not so Spry
And his Limbs are not as Supple
    As they were in years gone bye

But I cannot Now be Idle
    The few years that now Remain
Though my Heart is Full of sorrow
    And my Body Full of pain,
And I find myself oft musing.
    Oer the Changes of this life
Once I thought myself so favored
    I Had Children Friends and wife
Friends! No No I never Had them
    Though that name they long have Borne
They Have Flattered me in Sunshine
    To Betray me in the Storm
They Have Fled away and Left me.
    A much sadder wiser Man
But I'll profit by the lesson
    And Do all the good I can
And perhaps the clouds that Darkly
    Overshadow me to day
May be Rifted and the sunlight.
    May again Shine on my way
For a Hope still whispers to me
    ~~Ere I Close~~ this weary life.
I may still see Days of Sunshine.
    With my Children Friends and wife

A Call   1884

It was late I Had only Retired to my bed.
And Visions of slumber fast filling my Head
A Rap on my Door Guessing who can it be
A soft womans Voice is there Speaking to me

Come arise from thy slumber and gather I ..
Where sickness and sorrow thy services Need

It Has Taught me a Lesson while Life shall Remain
I will stand by the Bedside of sorrow and Pain
And the Calls of Humanity Ever shall be
In sickness and sorrow attend by me

I will go and God grant I a service may lend
To those who are needing in sorrow a Friend
For Ive Learned that a Friend is more precious then gold
And so Rare that their Value can never be Told

            Castle Valley   1883
Good Friends and Neighbors Everywhere
        Who want a New Location
Ill Tell you of the Nicest place
        There is in all Creation
Where You can make a pleasant Home
        Amongst good Honest Neighbors
In peace and Happiness Enjoy
        The Fruits of all your Labors
Then come my Boys who want a farm   arround the standard (Rally
And Bring your wives and littleones So Build us Castle Valley

Where sand is plenty coates too
        To use wherever you wish to
And in the mountains lots of wood
        The streams are full of fish too
Theres Timber on the Mountain side
        For Building and for Fencing
To Build the Bridges Make the Roads
        We now are just commencing
Chorus

Its not away in Mexico
        With Spaniards for your Neighbor
Nor Arizonas sultry Clime
        To swelter while you Labor
Nor Colorado where the snow
        Fills Every Nook and alley
But Here in utahs pleasant Vales
        Bright sunny Castle Valley
Chorus

This country Must be all Improved
        And that you May Rely on
Then come and Lend a Helping Hand
        To Build this part of Zion
Then if you want a Home come on
Thee is no Time to Dally
The Settlers just are coming in
        So Build up Castle Valley
Chorus

        The Faces on the Wall
They are looking Down upon me
        Those Dear Faces on the wall
They are Friends I Fony Have cherished
        Densly loved them one and all
They Have gone away and left me
        Almost Friendless and alone

Some are wandering o'er the Country
    Some to Foreign Parts have gone

Some are lying in the church yard
    Neath the cold and silent clay
Yet they seem to smile upon me
    As I gaze on them to day
There's my Mother speak it gently
    She was Very Dear to me
There's my Brothers and my Sisters
    Whom I never more may see

There's my wives Oh How I loved them
    Back Oh Back the starting tears
They have gone away and left me
    And I'm sad and lonely Here
There's my children Oh How sadly
    Are my Thoughts of them to Day
Some are lying in the church yard
    Some Have wandered Far away

Yet a few still linger near me
    On my Pathway shedding light
But our Little Band is Drifting
    Slowly Drifting out of sight
There are Friends I've fondly Cherished
    When this Life was in its Bloom
Some are Scattered o'er the Country
    Some are Resting in the Tomb

Yet They seem to smile upon me
    From their perch upon the wall
And the Tears are coursing Downward
    As their Names I now Recall

And my Heart is sad and Heavy
  As their Faces now appear
And I almost Feel their Presence
  And their Voices seem to Hear

But those Bright and Sunny Faces
  Who were once so Kind and Free.
They are Leaving me and Drifting
  Slowly Drifting from my View

    July 31ᵉʳ 1851   (July 31ˢ 1884.)

Oh yes my Boy this is a Day
  That I Remember well
And Shall on Each Succeeding year
  That I on Earth Shall Dwell
For on this Day Long years ago.
  The years were Thirty Three
Long we Had Traveled on the plains
  My Children wives and me
Long Long the way Oer Sandy plains.
  With Neither Feed or wood
And often Did we almost Faint
  For Water and for Food
But on this Day at Noon we Reached
  A clear and Running Stream
And on its Borders all along
  The Grass was growing green.
Away Here where White man never Trod
  To me was Born a Son
While we were on the Desert plains
  In Eighteen Fifty one

It seemed that a Law Had been Recently made
That a Tax on Polygamists Heads should be Laid
And in order to make them all glad to unmarry
The Tax was too Large for a Poor man to Carry

The Polygamists grumbled they said 'twas no use
'Twas unlawfull unjust it was termed abuse
To submit to such laws they would never be willing
And unless they were Forced to they would not Pay a shilling

The Rulers determined their scheme to pursue
Sent Lawyers and Marshals and Judges No few
And to Line all their Pockets sent plenty of Cash
Polygamy Now must go Down with a Smash

They started in Business arrested a few
They Tried them and Fined and Imprisoned them too
But they Stoutly Declared they would never unmarry
Although in the Prison they forced them too Tarry

So they tried a few more but with no better Luck
For they found the polygamists Being full of Pluck
They would stay there in Prison the Rest of their lives
Before they'd abandon their Children and wives

So they Kept up the scheme till the prison was Filled
And once in a while one was shot Down and Killed

But what Did they Care for their poor worthless Lives
When they would not abandon their Children and wives.

So they tried and acquitted the Shooter at once
To Shoot Down another when they got a chance
But they felt quite unsettled what next they should do.
For they found Every one to their families true

And although they would offer Free Pardon to such
Not one would acknowledge He was Married too much
So they Concluded to try to find some Little Flaw
To make it appears all Had Broken the Law

So that Congress would send out the troops Here in Haste
To Kill off the Mormons the Country Lay waste
To give them a chance to Inherit the Spoil
That the Mormons Had gained by their Labor and toil.

Now this is my Dream I have Told it to you
Am I a Sand Turned For Liberty can it be true
Or am I still Dreaming Ere long to awake
To find that my Dreaming was all a Mistake.

The Bachelors Hall

Ye Poet may sing of the trials and troubles
Of the man who must live with a Cross Scolding wife
And children who make the House look like a Stable
And always in Mischief to worry His Life

It is Nothing compared to the man who has Neither
And lives all alone in His Bachelors Hall
When He comes Home at night there's no light in the window
And no one to greet him or come at His call

He enters his cabin to over chairs stumble
He feels for the Matches in Darkness and gloom
They are not to be found So He swears and He grumbles
And wanders arround in the Dark Silent Room

At last a light kindled to satisfy Nature
He goes to the Cupboard for something to Eat —
A few crusts of Bread and a few cold potatoes
And Perhaps in the Corner Some scraps of cold meat

They soon are Brought out on an old Dirty Table
With Dishes as Dirty as Dirty can be
He sits Himself Down but to Eat He's not able
His apetite Craves Nothing there He can see

Then tired and Faint to the Bedside He glances
It is just as He left it this morning before
He puts out the light and to it advances
Gets under the covers and Days work is oer

But the Night is before Him to think of his sorrow
Alone and uncared for In Darkness and Dread
His slumbers are Broken and thin in the morrow
He Rises He almost could wish himself Dead

Then give me a wife though she scold me and vex me
And give me my Children their mischief and all
And give me my Friends though they often perplex me
And Take from my sight the old Bachelors Hall

    To Sister

Dear sister tis true I have not seen thy face
But to say that I love thee I feel no Disgrace

For Christ Has Commanded to Love one another
So I surely may give thee the Love of a Brother

Thy Heart Song ays Like a Book I have Read
Thou Hast sheltered the saints thou hast gave them Bread
Thou Hast opened thy Door to the servents of god
While they were Proclaiming salvation abroad

Now these are the words of the saviour to thee
If thou Hast Done it to them thou Hast Done it to me
Thy Deeds I have Known they have given me Joy
In a Land far away thou hast sheltered my Boy

Thou Hast friends Here in Zion who ever will Pray
That god in His mercy will open thy way
That Thou may,st be gathered with us find a Home
Your Friends Here in Utah Invite thee to come

Yes come to the Land where the House of the Lord
Is Opened to those who Have lived by His word
May Peace and content meet and Joy without End
Be thine while you live is the wish of your Friend

Childhood Again

Tis said that Fate Has so Decreed
    That when our Lives shall wane
And we have Gained a Ripe old age
    That childhood comes again

A Happy change if it will Blot
    The years that Lie Between
And give me Back my childhood Days
    As innocent as then

And Drive forever from my mind
  The sorrow and the Pain
And all the Cares and Ills of Life
  And Banish Every Stain

That lies Between these Childhood days
  That Memory Brings to me
When in that Dear old cottage Home
  Beside my Mothers Knee

If this can be Let childhood come
  I Hail the change with Joy
To Live again those Happy scenes
  As when I was a Boy.

But if those years must still Remain
  When Manhoods years are o,er
Then Lay me calmly in the grave
  Where sorrow comes No more

Why Did She Leave me

Why did She Leave me we Long were toyather
  Shareing the Joys and the sorrows of Life
Never assunder in Fair or Foul weather
  She was my Idol my own cherished wife
When we first met She was young and light Hearted
  I was in manhood Brave Hearted and bold.
Never a Thought we could ever be Parted
  Why Did she Leave me Because I am old

Many Long years we have Toiled on toyather
  Age Has come on and our childhood is past
Children arround us and grand children gather
  Wrinkles are Deep on my Forehead at Last

When in Her youth we were Happy togather.
    Fair as the Lilly and Pure as the snow
Pride and Base Flattery caused us to sever
    Now I must wander in Sorrow and woe
Dark are the clouds that arround me now Hover
    While I Remain in this Life Dark and cold.
Soon will the grave all my Loneliness covers
    Why Did She Leave me Because I am old.

Poetic

Yes when I have time I sometimes write a ryme
    For this is a Pleasure to me
And if I please others our Sisters and Brothers
    I dont see what Harm there can be
But if Im a Poet Im sure I dont know it
    Although Flatterers say it so
But in sending my name I shall Harbor no Blame
    Although in the waste Basket it go

Yet Longfellow shows He,s No Paitience with those
    Who By inspiration make Rhyme
But I do not agree with such fellows you see.
    It has Helped me yes many a Time
So my name I will send as I would to a Friend
    With a Hope it some service may be
But if not I will ask it Be thrown in the Basket.
    With others as Foolish as me

To Laura on the Death of Her Babe
Tis Hard to Part with those Dear Friends
    Weve loved and cherished Here
To lay them in the cold cold Grave
    How Bitter is the Tear
But when we think How short the time
    Ere weary life is oer
Then we shall meet with those we love
    To Dwell Forevermore

Oh may this be a Star of Hope
    To Help you Bear this pain
And Soothe the anguish of your Heart
    To Know you'l meet again
Oh what a Joy will then be yours
    On that Bright Sunny shore
Where Death and sorrow Cannot come
    And Parting is no more

To John West
Dear Friends once again we have met Here Togather
A Tribute of friendship to offer our Brother
Who with many others is called to go Forth
To Help in the Latterday Mission on Earth

Then let us Remember their names when we Pray
That god will Protect them while they are away
And keep Them from Sorrow Temptation and pain
Until they Shall Return back to Zion again

And now my Dear Brother to thee we will say
Be Faithfull and true and Forget not to pray
And Put trust in the Lord He will Ever be nigh
To Keep you From Evil your wants to supply

And altho the Dark clouds may be thick on your way
Remember that god is your Help and your stay
He will Raise you up Friends He will keep you from the
If you ask him in faith and will trust to His arm

We all shall Remember you oft in our Prayers
And ask Him to shield you from Danger and Snares
And keep you from sickness and Sorrow and Pain
Till you shall Return to your Kindred again

And when the time comes that your Mission is Done.
May you find many souls that your labors has won.
And Return to your Friends Brothers sisters and Mothers
Tis the wish of your Friends God Bless you our Brother

Sweet Des ret (June 20 years ago)

Sweet Deseret our Mountain Home
  We Hold thy memory Dear
Thy Birth Day we will celebrate
  On Each Succeeding year
We love thy Mountains and thy Hills
  Oer which the savage Roam
We love thy Vallies and thy plains
  Our Lovely Mountain Home

It is Just   years to Day
  Our Banner was Unfurled
On Ensign for our loyalty
  To Show to all the world
A little Band of Pioneers
  Had Oer the Desert come
And found the Place God Had Prepared.
  Our Lovely Mountain Home

Among the Rugged Snow capped Hills
    These Fertile Valleys Lay
Reserved to gather up the saints
    In this the Latter Day
Now saints from Every Land and clime
    Have to these Vallies come
To Build up Zion and to Share
    Our Lovely Mountain Home

The Twenty Forth Day of July
    We celebrate with cheers
In memory of those Valient men
    The Noble Pioneers
Who with their wives and Children too
    Our Desert Plains Did come
Until they Reached this pleasant land
    Our Lovely Mountain Home

And Here they Raised the Banner High
    The Stripes and Stars so Dear
And Here they Sent up Shouts of Joy
    To God who Led them Here
Since then Has Thousands gathered in here
    From Every Land they Come
To Dwell with saints of god and Share
    Our Lovely Mountain Home

The Saints Have made a paradise
  A lonely Mountain Home

And as the years Shall come and go
  While we Shall Dwell on Earth
Still may we Celebrate the Day.
  That gave our Home a Birth.
And may our Children yet unborn.
  For many years to come —.
Remember those Brave Pioneers.
  Who Found our Mountain Home

Stars and Stripes

Yes when we are courting the Ladies they try
To appear pure and Bright as the stars in the sky,
But it sometimes occurs when we make them a wife
That we find many Dark muddy stripes in their life

Then we find before marriage like stars they appear
But we find the Stripes tales which sometimes costs Dear
So tis true of some Ladies the stars Ere they wed
But stripes after marriage are Blue white and Red

My Lot —

My Lot is cast with those who Tread.
The Humble walks of life with Feet.
That oft are weary Begging Bread.
And Beistered with its Dust and Heat
I see around Those whose life
Is But a Dream of Joy untold
Who are free from want and care and strife
And all they touch soon Turns to gold
But all the story of my years
Is But a Tale of sighs and tears

And Has Her pets on whom to shower
Her favors and Her smiles unstayed.
And Frowns on others as they pass
And scatters Sorrow want and woe.
And Leaves no sunshine in their path
Through this Dark Life on Earth Below

For all the story of my years
Is but a tale of sighs and tears
It may be when this Life is over
To us a Happy change may come
When we Have Reached the other shore
Perhaps we'd find a better Home
And find the trials Here below
Our little faults Have chased away.
And those whose life was only Joy
Still have those little Debts to pay
Then all the story of my years
Will not be mixed with sighs and

I Have Friends among the children
I have Friends among the children
And I often see them Here
Their Merry Hearts and winsome ways
Bring to my Heart good cheer
They scatter Rays of sunshine
Around my lonely Home
And makes my Heart feel lighter
I am glad to See them come

Their peels of merry Laughter
Their Shouts of Joyous mirth

They make my lonely cabin
    A Brighter spot on Earth
But when I'm in my Cabin
    Deserted and alone
My thoughts will wander backwards
    To scenes long Past and gone

To Scenes of Pain and sorrow
    Too Dark for words to tell
When cruely Deserted
        By those I loved so well
By those whom I Had trusted
        And Cherished many years
They have left me in my Sorrow
    To waste my life in tears

To Manti   (Nov 18 1858)

The time Has Now arrived
    For us to Haste away
As Winter is approaching
        No longer Will Delay
Lest storms upon the Mountains
    Should Meet us on the way
            As we go over to Manti
We there shall meet our Friends
        In the Temple of the Lord
And for our Dead and living Friends
        Seek work with one accord
And there Receive the ordinances
            According to His word
                When we get over to Manti
So Peter Hitch your team up
    For you must Take the Lead

A Half a Dozen others now
    Are Ready to Proceed
For this Lateness of the Season
    Will Require a Little Speed
      As we go over to Manti'
So now we Have got Started
    And are Ready on our way
We are Far miles up the Canion
    Tis the Middle of the Day
Well Feed our Teams and Lunch awhile
    But must not Long Delay
      As we go over to Manti
About Fifteen miles Farther
    We Halted for the night
The snow was Gently Falling
    The Stars Had Hid their Light
But where we spread our Blankets
    The Fire was Burning Bright
      As we Went over to Manti
The next Day over the Mountains
    We traveled through the snow
While Baiting at the Coal beds
    The Chilley winds Did Blow
But still we traveled onwards
    To the Valey Down below
      As we went over to Manti'
There Here we seperated
    I went to Fountain green
To Visit with my Children
    For years I Had not seen
Two Days we Tarried with them
    A Happy Time I ween
      As we went over to Manti'

We then Resumed our Journey
    To Ephream there to find
Our Company awaiting us
    Whom they Had left behind
With other Friends who proved to be.
    So gentle and so Kind
        As we went ours to Manti'
One Sabbath Day we lingered
    Their Kindness we ded share
And then away to Manti'
    We Quickly Did Repair
And soon within the Temple
    We gained admission there
        When we got ours to Manti'
Two Happy Days we lingered
    In the Temple of the Lord
To work for Friends and Kindred
    And listen to His word
And then our Faces Homeward
    We Turned with one accord
        When we went ours to Manti'
Then we Hastened on ours Journey
    Lest Storms upon the Way
Should meet us in the Mountains
    And cause us Much Delay
But fortune seemed to Favor us
    And Kept the Storms at Bey
        As we come Home from Manti
There over the snow capped Mountains
    We Travelled on with Speed,
And Down the Rugged Canion
    With peties in the Lead
We Reached our Homes in Safely
    And glad was we indeed
        When we got Home from Manti

The Relief Society

You have asked me to meet with you all Here to day
And of course you Expect I'll Have something to say.
But I cannot Tell what youre Expecting of me
So Ile Say a few words of your Society

When our Numbers were few in the years past away
All the world was against us in that Early Day.
There were widows and Fatherless Needy and Poor
And the Sick and afflicted were near to our Door

It was then to the Sisters the Prophet made Known
There was work in the Kingdom for them Every one
They should Visit the sick they should Cheer up the Sad
They should comfort the sorrowing make their Hearts glad

They should clothe up the Naked the Hungry should Feed
And should comfort the saints wherever there was Need
This Mission He gave to the sisters and said
That the Blessings of Heaven Should fall on their Head

If Honest and faithfull and true they would be
And this is the Female Relief Society
Now sisters be Faithfull His words will be true.
And great is the Mission Entrusted to you

And great are the Blessings and Great the Reward
The Prophet Has said it and sure is His word
It is now Fifty years since this Mission He gave
He is now lying low in the cold silent grave
Yet His spirit has Ever a guide been to you
Since March Seventeenth Eighteen Forty two
So [illegible] will be [illegible] the [illegible]
[illegible]

Read at the 50th Anniversary of the Organization of the Relief Society. 1892

My 66th Birth Day

How swiftly Do the Years go Bye
    And Bear us Down the Stream
As age comes on they seem to fly
    And Vanish Like a Dream
It seems to me but Yesterday
    When Friends were gathered Here
To celebrate my Natal Day
    My Lonely Heart to cheer
And now again the Day Has Come
    And Tells Me one Year More
Has Past Away I'm sixty Six
    I'm Nearing to the Shore
And may I calmly Pass away
    When that Dread Hour shall come
Prepared to meet my Early Friends
    In our Eternal Home
And may I Hear those cheering words
    Thy Mission is well done
And thou Hast Gained with all thy Friends
    In Heaven a Happy Home

    A sentiment   (By A Collard)
My Sentiments are That while we are Here
We be of good cheer And Have Plenty of Beer
With Friends that are Dear But always Keep Clear
    As the Sky in a Bright sunny Day (A Collard)
    Reply
Your sentiments are Good I see

A Little Dance to Music sweet
And then Retire to Drink and Eat
The sisters then (God Bless them all)
Will Hunt their Baskets great and small
And soon the puddings cakes and Pies
Appear and Vanish Neath our Eyes
And then the Beer will welcome be
These are my Sentiments you see

A Toast (By J' ;)

The Seventies The Hunters and Fishers of this
Dispensation. May they get plenty of gas
May their Nets like Peters of old be Full to the

Geo W,

Will They Miss me

I am growing old and Feeble
And this life is Nearly over
And I soon shall cross the River
To that Bright and sunny shore
And I often Ponder over
All the years of life That I own
And the Question oft arises
Will they miss me when I'm gone

Yes they'l miss me from the office
When their Children may be Ill
And they want some simple Remedy
To save a Doctors Bill
They will miss me from the Tin Shop
When their Tins begin to Fail
And They find the water oozeing
From their Kettles pans and pails

And they find no one to mend them
They will also miss me there
They will miss me from the office
When they want some Printing Done
And they find no one amongst them
That Has learned the Press to Run

They will miss me from the work shop
When they want Hives for their Bees
That Have swarmed and have Collected
On the Branches of the trees
They will miss me from the seed Room
When they're wanting seeds to plant
And they want trees for the side walk
And the cash is getting scant

They will miss me on the Payment
When they meet Each Holiday
And they want a Recitation
Of the years long past away
They will miss me on the Evening
When they lea an Hour or two
For to listen to my Reading
Or to see the Magic show

They will miss me yes the children
When they come to visit me
They feel sad and lonely
When my Face no more they see
They will miss me all will miss me
Some for good and some for ill
But they all will soon forget me
When they lay me on the Hill

The Pioneers

God Bless those Hardy Pioneers
Who Banished from their Homes
Were led by His Directing Hand
To o'er the Desert come
Until they Reached this chosen land
Where white mans Foot Neer Trod
These Fertile Vallies in the Hills
Where they could Worship God
God Bless our Mothers and our Sires
Who for so many years
Have Toiled to Build His Kingdom up
Through sorrow and through Tears
The most Have worn their Bodies out—
And Resting By the way
Until He calls His Martyrs up
In that great coming Day
Then let us still Revere the Day
On which the Pioneers
Arrived within these Vallies where
They've Toiled so many years

June 13th 1881

Just thirty years ago to day
I left my Eastern Home
With wives and Children and with Friends
o'er Desert lands to Roam
Twas then I left my Mother Dear
Her Face to see no more
My Brothers Sisters and my Friends
So Dear, in Days of yore
I Bid adieu to all that Day
And started for the west

To seek a Home far o'er the plains
    Where while many feet now press
Where free from turmoil and from strife
    From Mobs and Tyrants Reign
I left my Friends and Home so dear
    And started o'er the Plains—
I took my wife to Share my fate
    I took my children three
To seek a Home in western lands
    They Bore me company
Six weeks we Traveled on the plains
    In Heading the Elk Horn
When in the Valley of the Platte
    Another Child was Born
Three months upon the plains we Toiled
    To Reach the Mountain Dell
And Oh the Hardships we Endured
    No Human Tongue can Tell
These Thirty years Have changed the Scene
    The young have all Grown old,
The old who have not Passed away
    Their fate will soon be told
The Desert where the wild Beast fed
    Now Blossoms like the Rose
And where the Red man Roamed the plains
    We Dwell in sweet Repose
The waving grain the tree the vine
    That now adorns the land
All shows to us we have been fed
    By His almighty Hand

The Kirtland Temple

Thou grand old Pile thy Fame is Spread
From land to land from sea to sea.

Where ere the gospel Light is shed
The saints have Heard or Read of thee

How oft in childhoods Happy Hours
Ere Thy Foundation stone was laid
Where thou art Reared with Dome and Tower
Upon that Very spot Ive Played

But Joseph spake the work began
And soon Thy Tower on High was Reared
There God again communed with man
There we Have oft His Name Revered

How oft within Thy walls we ve Heard
The meek and lowly Prophets Voice
And as we Listened to His word
Oh How it made our Hearts Rejoice

How oft within Thy walls we ve Met
To serve the Lord in praise and Prayer
And as we worshiped at His feet
How oft we ve Felt His Presence there

But Strangers pass its Portals Now
Yet oft my Thoughts will wander there
To where the Prophet oft Did Bow
Beneath Thy Roof in Humble Prayer

Joseph Smith the Prophet
You ask of me to sing a song
I fear I cannot do it
For I should Very Likely Fail
Before I d Half got through it

You ask me then to tell a yarn
    Well now I will Begin it
But when I'm Done I feel you'l say
    I'm sure there's nothing in it

A Subject I must study up
    To make a story of it
I think Ile take our early Days
    And Joseph Smith the Prophet .

He was a man of sterling worth .
    And True to Friend and Brother
And always Taught us to be True .
    And kind to one an other

He Told us ~~that~~ Pride and Haughtiness
    And Vanity were Evil
And all who would Indulge in them
    Were Prompted by the Devil

He Told us Fashions led astray
    And saints Should Never love it
That God Had made us in His Form
    And man Could not Improve it

He Taught us to Refrain From sin
    And Practice Good Behaviour
And Imitate the Pattern of
    Our meek and lowly Saviour

    My Sixty Seventh Birth Day
How swift the years pass out of sight
    And Bear us Down the Stream

As Speedy as the arrows Flight
  And Leaves us but a Dream
My Natal Day again Has come
  And I am Sixty Seven
How fast Im Nearing to my Home
  To meet my Friends in Heaven

Then grant oh god that I may Live
  My Mission to fullfill
And fit Myself to meet my Friends
  And in thy presence Dwell
And when my Time Shall come to go
  May all my work be Done
Then May I Calmly Pass away
  To Meet my Friends who are gone

A Sentiment
you ask of me a sentiment
  Well now you Have me caught
Ive Looked the Dictionary o'er
  And find it is a Thought
Well I Have Plenty of them Sure
  But cannot them Express
When I get up Before a Crowd
  To make a short address
But I will Try to Think a Thought
  And tell it Here to day
And if it Does not Please you all
  Just throw that Thought away
One Hundred Fifteen years ago
  God made this Nation Free
And on the Fourth Day of July
  Proclaimed Their Liberty

This great and glorious work was Done
    By His Directing Hand.
To Carry out His Glorious work
    On this His Chosen Land
Then Let us all with Happy Hearts
    Join in the Merry Throng
To celebrate this Glorious Day
    With Praises Dance and Song
And May we Have a Happy Time
    While we Together stay
And May no Jar or Discord come
    This Independence Day

Boyhood

I am Thinking I am Thinking
    Of the years Long Past away
Of my Bright and Sunny Boyhood
    When my Heart was Young and gay
Of my Father and my Mother
    Of my Brothers Sisters all
And the Times we used to gather
    In that Dear old Cottage Hall

I am thinking I am thinking
    When the Hollidays would come
How we Gathered Round the Table
    At the Dear old Cottage Home
Of the Pies and cakes and Puddings
    Of the Geese and Turkeys too
That would come from the Brick oven
    In the Kitchen Down below

And the Spare Rib Near it Roasting
    Swinging Round upon a wire
Of the Apples and the Cider
    That was warming on the Hearth
And the Merry peels of Laughter
    And the Happy Joyous Mirth

I am thinking I am thinking
    Of the Candy Joys and all
That was used to Fill our stockings
    That were Hanging on the Wall
When they told us that old Santa claus
    Would Down the Chimney creep
With Nice things to fill our stockings
    When we all were Fast asleep

I am thinking I am thinking
    Of the scenes long past away
And these Happy scenes still linger
    Of my Boyhoods Early Day
Though the scenes of Joy and sorrow
    And Lifes Changes all may be
Long Forgotten yet my Boyhood
    Will be Ever Dear to me

I am thinking I am thinking
    Of the snow flakes on my Hair
Of my Brow by age well Furrowed
    With the Marks of Toil and Care
Of my Feeble Limbs that tell me
    That my work is Nearly Done
I am waiting I am waiting
    For the Setting of the Sun

The Queen of the May

Dear Friends and Companions I'm Happy to meet you
With thanks for your Kindness and favors I greet you
And Hope we may all Spend a Happy May Day
As I shall in being the Queen of the May.

Then may no contention or Discord be Near
To mar our Enjoyment while we Remain Here
And may we be Happy while Here we shall Stay
Tis the wish of your Servent the Queen of the May
                                              Susie

I am Waiting

I am waiting at the Threshold
    I am weary faint and sore
I am waiting at the Threshold
    For the Opening of the Door
I am waiting at the Threshold
    Till the Master Bids me come
To the Glory that awaits me
    In that Bright and Happy Home

Oh the weary way I've Travelled
    Has been filled with Toil and Strife
Bearing Many a weary Burden
    Through this Dark and Stormy Life
But the Morning Now is Breaking
    And my Toil will Soon be over
I am waiting at the Threshold
    For the Opening of the Door.

Many Friends who Started with me
    Through this Dark and Stormy Life
One by one have Crossed the Threshold
    And are free from Toil and Strife

And I almost Hear the Voices
 Of the Friends whose Gone before
I am waiting at the Threshold
 For the opening of the Door

Oh How gladly will they greet me
 When my weary Toil is over
And have past beyond the River
 To that Bright and Happy shore
I have Borne a weary Burden
 Through this life of Toil and sin
I am waiting at the Threshold
 Till the Master Lets me in.

Cora

Patter Patter Little Feet
How I Love their Music sweet
In my arms I often fold
Little Cora two Years old
Little Dimples on Her cheek
Not a word she tries to speak
To my Heart I love to press
Little Cora Motherless
Quiet as a Little Mouse
She is Mistress of the House
And we Fully understand
By the movement of Her Hand
When she wants Her Little Nap
She will climb on Grandma's lap
Then Her coal Black Eyes will close
Soon She's lost in sweet Repose
May She Be as pure and good
All the way to woman hood
May all Blessings Earth can give
Rest upon Her while she live

Dear Friend who have Kind Thoughts of me
To Express them should you Feel Inclined
In this Book theirs a page where youth or old age
May jot Down what may be on their mind
A poem Inspered by the Muse
That comes From the Depth of the Heart
A Verse or a lay that your thoughts will convey
To your Friends your true feeling Impart
It will give much pleasure to Read
In the years that may chance to be mine
A Token thus penned By a Dear loving Friend
As I Totter Down lifes sad Decline

Dear Friend upon these pages white
There is a place for you to write
In Future years may I not find
Thy Name Beneath some thought of thine

Dear Friend these pages new so fair
Will soon be written Here and there
Amongst the Rest whose names I see
May I not find one thought from thee

As Down The stream of life you glide
May Friends be near on Every side
May Sunlight on thy pathway Shine
And Every Joy of Earth be thine

May the sunshine of life on your pathway be Bright
And your Heart by good actions be Happy and Light
Until crowned with old age you shall lie Down to Rest
Well knowing that all has been done for The Best

Dear girl be wise in choosing Friends
  Be certain they are true
Or when adversity shall come
  They'l Vanish Like the Dew
Soft words that fall from Flattering Lips
  Will Bring But Misery.
But He Who kindly tells ~~you~~ of ~~your~~ Faults
  Is But a friend to thee

Be true to yourself is a sentence oft spoken
It is written in Prose it is Sounded in song.
There is much of true wisdom contained in the sentence
If you are true to yourself you will never be wrong.
Then may you be guided by this little sentence
And never discard it for Pleasure or pelf.
For as on Lifes Journey you pass you will find it.
The Best of all counsel "Be true to yourself"

Dear Friend when I in future years
  Peruse this Book of mine
May I not find thy Name inscribed
  Beneath some thought of Thine
Should Fate our Paths in Life Divide
  That we should meet no more.
How sweet t'would be to think of Friends
  We Knew in Days of yore

May Peace content ment Joy and Love.
And Every Blessing from above
Repose within the Humble Cot
You call your Home Where the spot

These Leaves so White on which I write
　　Of Life an Emblem true
Let no foul Blot or Tarnished Spot
　　Be Found when written through

Who would Ever think a little Miss.
Would send to mee a Book Like this
unless She wished to Have a Laugh
To See my Funny Autograph
But Never mind my with Perhaps
Is Just as good as Younger Chaps
Who Talk and write their Flattery
God Bless you is my with For thee

This Book in its Rounds Has at last come to me
And I now must Expose what a noodle I be
But I will not Endevor to make up a Rhyme
For I surely would Fail So Ile not waste my time
But Ile do Something Funny to make you all Laugh
By writing Below Such a poor autograph

I cannot Beleve you are Jesting Dear Miss
In sending an Old man a Volume Like this
So may you gain wisdom in What I may Say
As the Snows of December Bury Flowers in may
Beware of the Flaterer Sharp is the Sting
And sorrow the Fruit to the Heart it will Bring
Tis a Friend who will Kindly Bring Faults to your View
Though He chide when you Err Hes no less Friend to you

Your Book lies open on the stand
The Pen with Ink is in my Hand
My mind is wandering Far away
To try to find a word to say
I want to wish you Happiness
A Pleasant life and joy and Peace
But cannot Bring it into Rhyme
So I must try another line
And if to you tis all the same
I'le give it up and write my Name
For then I know you all would laugh
To see my Funny Autograph
Before to you the Book I send
I'll scribble in it From your Friend

When Far away think over the past
Perhaps one Thought may be of me
Who lonely on this side world cast
Can Never cease to think of thee
A Flattering Tongue may Charm awhile
But will not stand the winters Chill
A Friend Through Storms and clouds will smile
And though Rough a Diamond still

A Rid...

Im a word of four letters though much to be wondered
If you take off my first you will take off one Hundred
      And the name of a fool will Remain
then my first take away Put my First back once more
You will Take off one Half that you took off before
      And the name of a Beast will be Plain
Put me back as at first then my first and my Secon
A Part of a firm Represents it so Reconed
      You will oft see it over the Door

My First second fourth Denotes Rank, it is said
My whole is a thing to be worn on the Head
   So now I will Tell you no more   Cowl

Changing Letters

Do you believe in an om_en_ She wrote on the Slate
No I Quickly Replied Tis a thing that I Hate
Then She wrote the last word with a _W_ Before
Then I Quickly Replied Tis a thing I adore
Then She said would you Like at the _alter_ to be
Then I added an _H_ Saying Lead me and See
Then She Quickly Replies if to you Tis the Same
I will Leave off the _H_ in Regard to my Name
Then She said I'll be _Hanged_ if I Try to please you
Then I added a _C_ Saying that you will do
Then She said would you Like for a _Ride_ to take me
I Replied yes with pleasure when I added a _B_
Then Let us be _Gone_ if your Ready says She
I am Ready I said if you Take off the _G_

Maxims

Never Leave cheerfulness Behind when you Enter a sick Room
Never Say yes when your better Judgment Says No
Never Tell your Best Friend all you know
Never Betray Trust or Confidence
Never seem one thing and act another
Never stoop to Flattery
Never wait for something to Turn up turn something up
The Cheapest thing is generally the Dearest
He who always his Bad Neighbors is generally
The worst Neighbor He Has
Those who Talk most Express the least good sense
It is cheaper to Buy than to Borrow
Friendship is Known by Deeds Not words

Kind words are as Easy spoken as Harsh ones
Plain words are Better than flattery
Truth and Honesty are always winners in the Race
Everything Begets its Kind so Love Begets love and Envy Envy
Religion is a garment for Every Day wear
Thoughts are our own Property
Words Belong to those who Hear them
Idleness is the Mother of Vice
Patience is the mother of Success
Firmness is the mother of Respect
Truth is the Mother of Honor
Industry is the mother of contentment
Intemperance is the Mother of crime
A Clear conscience is the Mother of Happiness

Rules for a sick Room

In Entering a sick Room Take Cheerfulness with you
Let your step be firm and your words be few But
Cheerful
Show no sign of Doubt or fear of the Result
Of what is Expected of you
Have no conversation in whispers in the
Presence of the sick
Let no word or Look betray a fear of
For the Patients safety
Keep a Cheerful Countenance
Consult Nature in all you do and if
you do not Know what to do do Nothing
It is better to Loose a Patient than to
Kill one
Have no more assistants than is Needed
As far as Possible Humor the Whims of the
Patient

Maxims for the Children

The Truth is Best in Every Case
A Falsehood always will Debase

Remember well The sabbath Day
Be sure you Neither work or play

A Place for Everything Prepare
When out of use be sure theyre there

If you've a job of work to do
Stick to it till you get it through

As soon as you are Done with play
Be sure to put your things away

Early to bed will Bring you Health
Early to Rise will Bring you Wealth

The Truth is always best to Tell
A Falsehood Never does as well

On Sunday Morning Neat and Clean
Be sure at Sabbath School yours seen

Talk not at The table Tis Vulgar, and Rude
For children to Talk unless asking For Food

You ma'es will tell all you know if yous wise
A gossip all your Honest people Despise

Work when you write and play when you play
But do Neither one on The Bright Sabbath day
when you have work to do then work
For your task you should not Shirk.

<u>At the Manti Temple July 4th 1893</u>

Oh tis Pleasant to Meet with our Friends Here to day
Whose Faces we have Known in the years Passed away
Who have toiled many years in the Kingdom of God
To scatter the News of Salvation abroad

And a few I behold who in years of ony ago
When the Prophet of God was here with us below
Who have Listened with Pride to the Prophets tongue
His words and itis Counsels will Ne er be forgot

But our Faces are wrinkled ours Hair turning Grey
Our Feeble Limbs tell us we are Passing away
But as long as we live let us stand by the Truth
That we learned from his Lips in the Days of our youth

That when we have finished our Mission below
We may meet Him again beyond sorrow and woe
There to finish the Mission He left for us here
That our Crown may be Bright He will give us to wear

            At Home   July 4th 1894
      Dear Children once again The Muse
        Is whispering unto me
      It Bids me seat myself and write
        The subject is of Thee
      I feel so lonely and so sad
        As time goes swiftly By
      It Plainly tells me that the End
        Is Swiftly Drawing Nigh

But Never think to call on me
    An hour to Pass away
To cheer a Heart that once like yours
    Was Thoughtless and as gay
But age comes on and Busy life
    With me is in the Past
And Friends of youth I loved so well
    Have Turned away at last

And now alone I Bide my time
    Till god shall Bid me come,
To leave this sad and lonely life
    To Find a Better Home
There I shall meet my Early Friends
    I loved so well in youth
Who, ve toiled and wore their Bodies out
    To spread the Cause of truth

Backward Turn Backward

Backward Turn Backward Oh time in your Flight
Make me a Child again Just for tonight.
Place me again on my Dear Mothers Breast.
Free from the Cares of this life let me Rest
Let me again see the smile on her Face
While She with Rapture her form will Embrace
In Her dear arms For a time let me Rest
Forgetting the sorrows that now ? is my Breast.

Take me again to the Home of my Birth
With Friends & with Kindred arround the old Hearth
There let me wander o.er Meadows & hills
Over the wild woods & Murmuring Rills
Now Reining Dolly to Plow out the corn
Till I hear the Sweet sound of the old Dinner Horn
And then to the Kitchen where Mothers Presides
With apitite Enoying the Food She Provides

The sweetest and best of all Dainties on Earth
Prepared by our Mothers in the Land of our Birth
There in the Corner The Brick oven Stands
Brim full of Dainties all made by her hands
There are Puddings & Cakes and Bread made of Rye
And The Dearest of all is The Old Pumpkin Pie
Then Backward Turn Backward O Time in your flight
Make me a child again Just for tonight.

Our Family
My Mother Sixteen Children had
    She Raised them all but one
She Left Him Dying in New york
    His Darling Little Son
The Next at Kirtland on the Hill
    Four graves are Dying there
Two Brothers and two Sisters Dear
    Have Slept for many a year
At Macedonia Illinois
    Another Brother Died
Just as to Manhood He had come
    He was our Mothers Pride
And Then at Nauvoo there we Left
    Another Sister Dear

We laid Her in the Silent grave
. Our Father too is there
And then at Kanesville Iowa
. A sister Drooped and Died.
We laid Her Neath the Cold Cold clay
. With Mother By Her side
At Salt Lake city there we left
. Two sisters lying there
Beneath the Cold & silent clay
. They've slept for many a year
Our oldest Brother many years
. Has slept Neath Dixie soil
And still another Farther south.
. Is Resting from his Toil
One sister and three Brothers still
. Of all that little Band
Though many Many miles apart—
. Are still upon the Sand
The Rest are sleeping by the way
. They're Free from toil & Pain
Until the Reserrection Day.
. Then we shall meet again

The Millenium
This world is not so bad a world.
. As many people make it
Tis just as good and just as bad
. As we poor Mortals make it
If all the people in the world
. Would do unto Each other

And Hatred would be turned to Love.
And all our troubles Vanished
The Time that now is Spent in crime.
Would then be Spent in labor
And Each one then would be as Rich
And Happy as His Neighbor
The Time that's Spent in Hunting Crime
The Time thats Spent to do it
The Time that is spent to Punish crime
And all thats wasted through it
If it was spent in Honest toil
And doing good to others
We'd all be rich and all be wise
And live Like Honest Brothers
One Half the world now follow crime
For wealth or Pride or Passion
The other Half with Honest toil
Support them in that Fashion
It will be thus until the Day
Of final Seperation
The wicked then will be Destroyed
The Righteous Rule the Nation

Feb 19th 1899 My Seventy fourth Birth day
How Swiftly glide the years away
Adown lifes turbed stream
So fleet One year ago to day
To me is but a dream

My Life.   at. 73. =

I am sitting alone in my Cabin Today
I am thinking of years that have long passed away
They are three score and Ten with the adding of three
Which the Lord in his mercy has given to me

They Embrace all The years that the prophet of god
Proclaimed the glad news of salvation abroad
with His Snares and Toils Persecution and woes
Till He finished His work and was slain by His foes

They Embrace all the sorrows the Joys and the fears
That the Saints have Endured in those forty nine years
Since Driven by mobs over the Desert to Roam
On the tops of these mountains to find a new Home

They were years of great sorrow of labor and Toil
Subduing the savage Reclaiming the soil
While we built up new Homes over mountains and Vale
Where Naught but the savage and wild Beast did Dwell

But these years are all Past and our labor is Done
We have finished the work that in youth we began
For our children we found a Bright sun in its west
But for us all its Rays are laid Down in the west